"WHAT'S SO FUNNY ABOUT ME DRIVING YOU HOME?" Russ asked.

At first he didn't think Tory was going to answer. Then he caught a glimpse of her face in the light of a nearby streetlamp, and he could have sworn she was blushing.

"You must have known I had a crush on you in high school," she murmured.

"Did you?" He felt ridiculously pleased.

"Oh, yes," she assured him. "Big time. And to the teenage girl I was, dinner tonight and then—be still my beating heart—you driving me home, well, that would have made all my teenage dreams come true."

Although her tone was light, Russ sensed more than a little genuine emotion behind her words. "I wish I'd known how you felt back then."

"No, that would have been too humiliating," she said quickly. "You might not have meant to be cruel, but you'd have laughed your head off at mousy Vicki MacDougall lusting after the big basketball star."

"Teenage boys aren't noted for their sensitivity," he said.

"Besides," she added, "I heard your dates got more than dinner and a ride home." As soon as she said it, she looked stricken. "Can I take back that last part?"

Russ had never been able to resist a challenge, especially one issued by an attractive girl. "So," he teased, "exactly how would this dream date of ours have ended?"

He didn't give her time to answer, sure he knew what it would be. Instead, he tugged her close, and leaned in to bring his lips to hers in a playful kiss, just between friends. Or so he thought until his mouth actually touched hers. . . .

WHAT ARE *LOVESWEPT* ROMANCES?

They are stories of true romance and touching emotion. We believe those two very important ingredients are constants in our highly sensual and very believable stories in the LOVE-SWEPT line. Our goal is to give you, the reader, stories of consistently high quality that may sometimes make you laugh, sometimes make you cry, but are always fresh and creative and contain many delightful surprises within their pages.

Most romance fans read an enormous number of books. Those they truly love, they keep. Others may be traded with friends and soon forgotten. We hope that each LOVESWEPT romance will be a treasure—a "keeper." We will always try to publish

LOVE STORIES YOU'LL NEVER FORGET
BY AUTHORS YOU'LL ALWAYS REMEMBER

The Editors

Loveswept ®913

THAT SPECIAL SMILE

KATHY LYNN EMERSON

BANTAM BOOKS
NEW YORK · TORONTO · LONDON · SYDNEY · AUCKLAND

THAT SPECIAL SMILE

A Bantam Book / November 1998

ISBN 0-553-44644-4

Published simultaneously in the United States and Canada

Bantam Books are published by Bantam Books, a division of Bantam
Doubleday Dell Publishing Group, Inc. Its trademark, consisting of the
words "Bantam Books" and the portrayal of a rooster, is Registered in
U.S. Patent and Trademark Office and in other countries. Marca Regis-
trada. Bantam Books, 1540 Broadway, New York, New York 10036.

PRINTED IN THE UNITED STATES OF AMERICA
OPM   10 9 8 7 6 5 4 3 2 1

For Amie

ONE

"Daddy, I want to be in a beauty pageant."

Russ Tandy stared at his twelve-year-old daughter, thinking that he couldn't possibly have heard correctly. But Amanda's clear brown-eyed gaze was calm and disturbingly serious. When her late mother had gotten that look in her eyes, he'd always known he was about to lose the coming battle.

Two customers were browsing the shelves of Tandy's Music and Gifts, the small Waycross Springs shop that had been in Russ's family for three generations, but neither seemed to need his services at the moment. He was free to focus on the golden-haired child gazing hopefully at him from the other side of the counter.

When had she gone and grown up on him?

Amanda had inherited Melody's baby-fine blonde hair rather than his thick, reddish-brown curls. But Russ's daughter had gotten her height from him. She was going to be tall and willowy. Like a model, he realized with a sense of shock.

"What brought this on?" he asked, trying to conceal that his first reaction was wholly negative. He knew very well what would happen if he flat out said no. Amanda would dig in her heels, stick out her lower lip, and pout. He'd have to find some tactful way to discourage this appalling new whim.

"The Miss Special Smile competition is going to be held at the Sinclair House," she said, naming the grand old nineteenth-century hotel that was the linchpin of economic prosperity in their small, rural Maine community. "It's a great opportunity."

Not what he'd asked, Russ thought, but he realized Amanda's response was probably the closest thing to an answer he was going to get. He hoped his daughter wasn't developing Melody's knack for evasion.

A bell above the door tinkled musically as a young couple, plainly tourists, entered the shop. "Stay put," he said to Amanda. "We'll talk in a minute."

Waycross Springs was a resort for most of the year, offering cool mountain air as an escape in the summer and skiing in winter. The third boom time was in progress at the moment as nature presented its annual display of brilliant fall foliage. Leaf-peepers filled every hotel, motel, and bed-

and-breakfast in the area. Enough of them wanted to buy souvenirs to take home with them to ensure that the Tandys stayed in business year after year.

After he waited on the customers, selling them postcards and, as a nice bonus, one of the tiny pewter figurines he stocked, he turned his attention back to his daughter. She'd come behind the counter and was shifting impatiently from foot to foot. He doubted she'd changed her mind about this beauty-pageant business during the interim. He wasn't that lucky.

Trying a new tack, he asked, "How did you hear about the competition?"

At once she brightened, smiling up at him as pride filled her expression and her voice. "I got a personal invitation from the pageant organizers."

Russ frowned. Someone had dared solicit a child? The very idea made him see red, but he swallowed the urge to explode and forced himself to keep his voice level. "May I see it?"

Amanda promptly opened one flap of the backpack in which she carried her books. She'd stopped by the store after school, as she did every weekday. Along with a small packet of Oreo cookies, she produced a legal-size envelope addressed to Miss Amanda Tandy at their street address in Waycross Springs.

That made Russ stop and ponder, for it indicated that the origin of this "opportunity" might have been Amanda herself and some form or contest entry she had filled out. There was no door-to-door delivery in their tiny town. Everyone had a post office box or a rural route number. The local postmaster had those memorized, and although he was supposed to return misaddressed mail to the sender, he rarely did so, simply popping it into the correct box instead. Just this once, Russ wished he'd been less obliging.

Inside the envelope was a form letter on good-quality business stationery, together with an application and a permission slip for him to sign. The pageant was scheduled right before Thanksgiving. The deadline for entering was a little more than a week away.

"I have to send this in," Amanda told him, taking all but the letter from his hand. "And I have to go to a personal interview before I can be accepted." Her voice trembled with barely contained excitement and she scarcely seemed able to keep from bouncing up and down as she waited for him to finish skimming the letter directed to "Dear Candidate." He took in only about half of what it said. "Can I enter, Daddy? Pleeeease!"

"I need to think about this, honey." Though most of his attention was on Amanda and her earnest request, he was distracted by the movements of the others in the shop. Mrs. Benning, the piano teacher, had been browsing for an hour. Tim Latterly, the game warden, was trying to decide between a Madonna CD and one featuring Celine Dion.

"But, Daddy—"

"You know how hard it is to discuss serious matters when I'm working."

"Oh, Daddy. Just say yes. It's no big deal." Amanda wasn't ordinarily a manipulative child, but there was now a distinct whine in her voice. Once again she reminded him of Melody. Uneasy with the comparison, he looked up with relief as one of his customers approached the counter.

"We'll talk about it tonight. At home. Want to wait on Mrs. Benning, Amanda?" She'd always enjoyed working the cash register. She'd "helped" at the store from the moment she'd been old enough to know which keys to press.

"I *want* to be in the beauty pageant," she muttered, but she climbed up on the high stool in front of the register, took the sheet music, rang up the sale, and bagged the purchase and receipt.

Her smile for Mrs. Benning looked forced. No surprise there. Following in Russ's footsteps, Amanda had attempted to learn to play the piano. Like him, she'd hated it. The musical talents of the Tandy family were directed toward mastering a somewhat less common instrument.

"I already have a picture to put on the brochures," Amanda announced.

Brochures? What brochures? Russ scanned the letter once more and found the reference. Contestants were encouraged to print brochures in order to solicit sponsors.

Ask for money, in other words, to pay an entry

fee. His blood pressure rose when he saw they expected Amanda to cough up four hundred dollars just to get into this foolish competition.

"Such a pretty girl," Mrs. Benning said as Amanda handed over her package. "Pretty as a picture." She beamed at both Russ and Amanda before walking away.

Something clicked at this second reference to pictures. That had to be it, the source of the letter. Just before school started, Amanda had gone to a photography studio with her best friend, Jolene, for what Jolene's mother had called a "girls' day out." Russ had been livid when he'd seen the resulting portrait of his little girl. Going for glamour, the photographer had made Amanda look at least sixteen. Entirely too grown up. She'd had an almost . . . knowing expression in her eyes. And she'd been dressed in a tuxedo.

He'd hated that photograph at first sight, but of course he hadn't let Amanda know. She'd been so tickled with her new look she'd come home still sporting the makeup and the elaborately styled and sprayed hair. He'd swallowed his first reaction, to demand the name of the person who'd made his baby look like a cheap hooker, and mumbled something about how she certainly did look different. He'd been tremendously relieved when she'd washed all that gunk off her face and out of her hair.

Russ struggled to keep his voice casual and tried to remember what else Amanda had told him about their outing. "Did Jolene get an invitation too?" he asked.

For a moment Amanda looked almost guilty. "Jolene thinks beauty pageants are stupid."

Bless Jolene, Russ thought. He didn't voice that heresy aloud, however. If he was reading the signs right, the two girls had already had a falling-out over Amanda's desire to become a beauty queen.

"Are you still going to her house this afternoon?" he asked cautiously. Jolene and Amanda normally did their homework together there after school, until he closed the store and picked up his daughter on his way home.

"I guess," Amanda said.

"Jolene has a right to her opinion," he reminded her.

"I guess."

Seeing the forlorn expression on his daughter's face, Russ decided he'd better do a bit of investigating before he refused her request. He'd need a carefully reasoned explanation when he said no. He told himself he'd raised a sensible child. Surely she'd see the light if he was patient enough to marshal compelling arguments, especially if he had Jolene on his side.

There were times, Russ thought, when it would be much easier if he were the kind of parent who simply laid down dictates and expected to be obeyed. He'd never dealt that way with Amanda, though, and he wasn't about to start now. He didn't spoil her, even if she was the apple of his eye.

He didn't deny her much, either.

A Madonna CD landed on the counter, along with a twenty-dollar bill. Once again, Amanda rang up the sale, but as soon as Tim Latterly was out of the store, just when Russ might have initiated further discussion of the pitfalls of entering contests, she slid down off the stool and wrapped her arms around his waist.

"I really, really want to do this, Daddy," she declared, and rested her cheek against his chest.

Russ sighed, staring down at the top of her golden head where it nestled close to his heart. "Can you tell me why entering a beauty pageant is suddenly so important to you?"

Obviously quoting from the letter he'd tossed onto the counter, she said, "It's a character-building experience."

"And?"

"And one of the prizes is a thousand-dollar scholarship."

At least that made some kind of sense. When she turned ten, Amanda had announced she wanted to be a marine biologist. She'd been looking at college catalogs ever since. The colleges she liked all had one thing in common. They were expensive.

He ruffled her silky hair, then set her away from him. "We'll talk about it tonight," he promised. Her smile was so radiant that he didn't stop to think before he added, "Mrs. Benning is right. You're pretty enough to win any beauty contest."

"Daaaaddy! It's not enough to be pretty. I have to be talented too. And I have to answer questions in front of hundreds of people."

In Waycross Springs? Maybe in summer or during ski season, but this competition was being held at a time of year when only the contestants' families were likely to show up. With any luck, Russ thought, he wouldn't be among them.

"Better get going," he said. "Jolene will wonder where you are."

Amanda threw herself back into his arms, hugging him tightly. "I'll make you so proud of me. I'm going to win. I'm sure of it."

"Whoa! Wait a second. I haven't agreed to anything."

But Amanda wasn't listening. She released him and dashed toward the door, calling back over her shoulder that she'd see him later. Shaking his head, Russ watched through the plate-glass display window as she raced off down the sidewalk, darting between two tourists and nearly upending a recycling bin.

Typical Amanda-the-whirlwind, he thought. All of this was. As soon as she was out of sight, he returned to the counter and reached for the phone. Beva Scott, Jolene's mother, answered on the second ring. Russ knew her to be a forthright, honest person and a loving wife and mother, always ready to share a laugh or a cup of coffee—

and she made the finest coffee in Waycross Springs. More than once, Russ had thought he should have been smart enough to marry such a woman.

"What do you know about this Miss Special Smile pageant?" he asked after he'd identified himself.

After a short exchange of information, Beva acknowledged that his guess was likely correct. If Amanda hadn't had that photograph taken, the pageant organizers would probably never have gotten her name.

"I hold you responsible, Beva," Russ said. He wasn't entirely kidding. "Looks to me like you're the one who got me into this mess."

"Oh, no. I'm not buying into any guilt trips." Good-natured laughter traveled to him over the phone line, making him smile in spite of himself. "For one thing, that photographer actually managed to make me look good. And for another, having our pictures taken wasn't even my idea."

He heard her make a small sound, almost a gasp.

"You okay?"

"Just taken with a thought. Listen, Russ, there may be a better person than me to help you out. I'll tell you more when you come for Amanda. Got to go." She hung up before he could respond.

In between customers, Russ made two more phone calls. The first was to the Sinclair House, where the director of public relations confirmed what Beva had told him about the Special Smile competition. Even though he'd never heard of the contest, it seemed it was a reputable one that did indeed offer college scholarship money, among the prizes. Just to be sure, he next phoned the Waycross Springs Police Department to talk to his brother, Gordon.

By the time Russ closed the store at six, he knew a fair amount about the pageant. That was the good news. The bad news was that, so far, he hadn't come up with a single logical reason to deny his daughter's request to participate.

Tory Grenville wiped grimy hands on her thighs, leaving dark streaks on already dirty blue jeans, and regarded the tiny vegetable garden with satisfaction. Here it was, only midafternoon on Saturday, and already the last of the potatoes, carrots, and onions filled the wicker basket her mother had always used for the harvest. True, Tory had let some of the produce go by, and an astonishing number of weeds were flourishing in the little plot, but she had grown enough veggies to make a nice pot of homemade stew. Even though it was going to mean eating late, she'd make it that day, enjoy some for supper, and freeze the rest. Just contemplating the whole process made her feel remarkably domestic.

"Yuck," she muttered to herself. "Next thing

you know, I'll be turning into a damned home-body."

She carried the heavy basket into the house, which still smelled of lemon furniture polish from that morning's weekly cleaning binge. She liked sensing tangible proof of her accomplishments, at home and in her job. She also tended to hoard every word of praise, each pat on the back, as if they were gold stars on school papers. It was a failing, she supposed, but one she could live with. One, in fact, that helped her maintain a positive outlook, something not always so easy to do, especially this past year.

A five- by eight-inch lined tablet on the kitchen counter contained Tory's list of "things to do" before she left on her next business trip. Most were already checked off, but one that remained was: *Call Beva about feeding cats*. Since she would be away for four days, she didn't want to leave her pets completely on their own.

She was reaching for the phone when it rang. "What are you, psychic?" she asked when she recognized Beva's voice.

Beva laughed, listened to Tory's request that she look in on Dichotomy and Paradox, otherwise known as Dick and Pat, and readily agreed to take on the responsibility.

Tory had first run into Beva in the grocery store. Literally. Their carts had collided at the end of the pet-food aisle. Beva's sack of dog food, balanced precariously on top of her fully loaded cart, had gone flying, burst open, and covered the floor with kibble. By the time they'd stopped laughing and helped the stock boy clean up the mess, they'd become fast friends.

"So why were you calling me?" Tory asked.

"Remember my daughter Jolene's friend Amanda? The one who went to our session at the photographer's with us?"

"Sure."

A pretty girl, with brown eyes and blonde hair. Tory remembered both the child and the day very well. They'd had a lot of fun primping and posing and playacting for the camera. The photography studio had provided the clothes. Costumes, really. And the photographer, a strange little person named Alexa, employed a full-time makeup person and hairstylist.

"What about Amanda?" Tory asked when Beva didn't say anything more. What sounded like a small bell jingled in the background. Tory frowned. Her friend cut hair for a living and had a small shop attached to her home, but that door had a buzzer, not a bell.

"I called to tell you—warn you, really—that Amanda's father is on his way over to talk to you. I'm minding his store for him so he can."

That explained the bell, but left a greater mystery unsolved. "What on earth does he want with me?"

"He thinks you may be able to help him out, since I told him how much Amanda liked you. I sort of hinted that she might listen to your advice."

Sort of hinted? "Are you nuts? She's a nice kid and all, but we barely exchanged a dozen words the whole day."

Kids, as far as Tory was concerned, were an alien species. Amanda and Jolene had giggled throughout the photo session and spent the rest of the time whispering together. Tory smiled. Come to think of it, she and Beva had done a lot of giggling and whispering themselves.

"Ooops," Beva said. "Another customer just came in. Wing it, will you? And try to help. Russ Tandy's a friend of mine, and a heck of a nice guy."

"Russ Tandy?" Tory yelped, but she was speaking to dead air.

Numb, she hung up.

Russ Tandy was about to arrive on her doorstep?

Russ Tandy, the boy she'd had such a wicked crush on for all four miserable years of high school?

That Russ was Amanda's father made perfect sense, but Tory hadn't connected the dots on the day they'd gone to the photographer's studio. After all, there were lots of Tandys in Waycross Springs. The town had been founded a couple hundred years back by the Tandys and the Sinclairs and the Meads. Tory's family, the MacDougalls, had been latecomers, arriving by way of

Canada in the late nineteenth century to work in the nearby mill town of Moreton Falls. The Scotts had come even later. Beva, she realized, probably didn't realize Tory was this town's prodigal daughter.

Not that it mattered.

If Russ was Amanda's father, there must be a Mrs. Tandy, Amanda's mother. Tory couldn't help but feel a twinge of jealousy. Then she had to laugh at herself. Like she really thought he'd been pining away all these years, waiting for her to come back! He'd never even noticed her in high school. He'd been the big basketball star. She'd been the class brain.

Her doorbell rang. Her breath stopped.

"I can do this," she whispered.

He wasn't an eighteen-year-old heartthrob now. And she was no longer the shy, skinny girl who got red-faced and tongue-tied every time she tried to talk to any boy, let alone a dreamboat extraordinaire like Russ Tandy.

She could talk to him. She would talk to him. She'd long since mastered the art of presenting a calm facade to the world. He'd never know she was quaking inside as badly as the most self-conscious adolescent.

She took a step toward the hallway and stopped, remembering how she was dressed. She knew it shouldn't matter that she was wearing tattered, grubby jeans and a baggy sweatshirt, or that she had pulled back her unruly hair with a coated rubber band without bothering to look at the result in the mirror, but a sigh escaped her anyway.

The doorbell sounded again, and Tory reminded herself she was appropriately garbed for what she'd had to do that day. She hadn't expected anyone to come calling at the house she'd taken over from her parents a few months earlier. She'd only reconnected with one or two old friends since she'd been back in Waycross Springs. About the only person she saw regularly was Beva.

At the door, she slid the frothy white curtain aside far enough to peer out. It was the same Russ Tandy all right.

He'd aged well. No excess fat clung to his tall, lean frame and he still had that gorgeous head of hair, thick and naturally curly. Every girl in Waycross Springs High School had longed to tangle her fingers in that mass of cinnamon-colored ringlets.

Shape up, Tory! she warned herself.

Still, her heart was racing, and by the time she put her hand on the doorknob and turned it, she feared she'd melt into a puddle at his feet the moment he spoke to her.

"Ms. Grenville?" he asked when she opened the door. His voice was better than she'd remembered. Deep and a bit gravelly. The kind of voice a woman couldn't help wanting to hear in the dark across a shared pillow.

She nodded in response to his question, finding speech beyond her as she looked up into the familiar, handsome face. Even breathing was a bit difficult. Her chest felt tight, her pulse was erratic. Only the obvious fact that he was unaware they'd ever met before kept her from slamming the door closed and running upstairs to hide under the bedcovers. Anything to spare her this agony. It was as if she'd suddenly been flung back into the worst insecurities of her teen years.

"Are you all right?" he asked.

Form the words. Speak the words, she ordered herself.

"Yes," she managed. "I'm just out of breath."

Apparently she sounded normal enough. At least he didn't translate "out of breath" into breathless.

"I'm Russ Tandy," he said. "I believe you know my little girl, Amanda. I'd like to talk to you about her for a moment if I may."

Act normal. He's nothing to you. You're all grown up now.

It seemed easier to let him go on believing she was a stranger.

"Please. Come in." Tory stepped back to allow him to pass into her house.

He smelled of Old Spice and fresh air and leather, the latter from a stylish long coat he was removing to reveal a dress shirt and tie. What he wore at work, she supposed. The shirt was pale yellow, patterned in subtle green and brown stripes. The tie had an equally conservative design, a brocadelike texture on a dark brown background.

She tracked him with her eyes as he turned to enter her living room, her gaze dropping briefly to admire the hint of a firm backside and powerful thighs beneath loose pleated trousers. She still felt a bit dazed, but once he'd moved ahead a few feet, putting much-needed distance between them, her equilibrium slowly returned. She ordered herself to stop mentally drooling over the man.

No cause for panic, she thought when she'd managed that not inconsiderable feat. He didn't even know who she was.

He'd come about his daughter.

She gestured toward a chair and took the sofa at a right angle to it. The facade she presented to the world, her business persona, snapped firmly into place. She gave him a polite smile, and her voice was steady as a weather vane on a calm day.

"What can I do for you, Mr. Tandy?"

Before he could answer, Dick and Pat came barreling into the room. Dick, a short-haired tabby, stopped short at the sight of a stranger and went airborne, reversing course in mid-jump. Pat, always the braver of the two, approached at a more cautious pace to sniff the intruder's black leather shoes.

"You've passed inspection," Tory informed him as the black-and-white Maine coon cat lost interest and strolled away.

Russ grinned and her heart turned over. He'd

lost none of the charm he'd possessed as a teen-ager. Worse luck!

Clearing her throat, she managed to return his smile. "You mentioned your daughter?"

Other questions flashed through her mind, unspoken. She knew now what store Beva must be minding. The Tandys had always run the same business. But she didn't have a clue whom Russ had married or why Mrs. Tandy wasn't the one talking to her.

"I have a favor to ask," he said, and now it was his turn to appear ill at ease.

She waited and in the short silence gave herself permission to appreciate the strong line of his jaw, the small laugh lines inscribed around his eyes, the tiny twitch at one side of his mobile mouth that hinted he was capable of self-mockery.

"This is more difficult than I'd imagined," he confessed. "You don't know me from Adam. But Beva Scott thought . . . that is, we . . ."

"Just spit it out," she suggested bluntly, afraid that if he stayed much longer she'd lose her hard-won composure. "Or perhaps you should ask your wife to talk to me."

Her words were an attempt to remind herself how futile any lustful thoughts about Russ Tandy were, but as soon as they were spoken, she knew she'd said the wrong thing. He froze. His expression went blank. He almost ceased to breathe for an endless moment before he said, softly, "My wife died when Amanda was eight."

"I'm sorry." The words were automatic. So was her internal reaction. Four years? And he still reacted this strongly? There might not be a wife in the picture any longer, but the sainted memory of a devoted spouse seemed just as high a barrier.

Fool, she chided herself. Like it matters? Russ Tandy wasn't sitting in her living room because he'd come to ask her out on a date, though she suspected that possibility had occurred to Beva, their mutual friend. He was there because of Amanda.

"I need help with my daughter," he said, once more confirming that fact. "Because she had such a glamorous picture taken, the day you and Beva Scott and Beva's daughter visited the photography studio in Three Cities, Amanda has now decided she wants to be a beauty queen. There's a pageant here late next month. At the Sinclair House. Two days ago she told me she wants to enter."

Tory blinked at him, confused. "Why come to me? I don't know anything about beauty pageants."

He couldn't, she thought, possibly guess how she'd once fantasized about the annual televised events. It had been a brief phase, a passing fancy. She'd soon realized how sexist and politically incorrect such competitions were and convinced herself that she had never seriously contemplated entering one. Good thing, too, since she wasn't exactly beauty-queen material.

He cleared his throat, so hesitant and uncomfortable that Tory began to feel sorry for him. Now, there was a role reversal! She might have enjoyed his discomfort more, however, if he hadn't attempted to explain the reasoning behind his decision to contact her.

"I figure you're responsible, at least in part," he told her. "You came up with the idea of having those portraits taken, and that led directly to Amanda's sudden yen to compete."

Her eyes narrowed. "You blame me because your daughter thinks she's pretty enough to enter a pageant?"

"She never noticed her own appearance before the photo shoot."

Reminding herself he was a concerned father, and that he probably had no clue he was being insulting, she kept sarcasm at a minimum. Fingers clasped around her knees, she boldly met his gaze. "What, exactly, do you think I should do to make up for this heinous crime?"

He angled himself toward her, any doubt he might have had apparently a thing of the past. Enthusiasm shone in his dark, expressive eyes. Self-confidence radiated from his every hunky pore, but this time Tory was pleased to find she did not immediately succumb. His preposterous accusation had managed to counteract the effect of his charisma. Her earlier nervousness was fast disappearing.

"Beva suggested you'd be a good person to

give Amanda some pointers," Russ confided. "I—"

A very unglamorous snort escaped her. The idea was so absurd that just considering it overrode the last vestiges of her shyness around him.

"Take a gander, Russ." She stood, sweeping both hands down her body from breast level to hip and back up again. "Does this look like someone who's an expert on beauty pageants?"

TWO

Russ's fascinated gaze lingered on every feminine curve.

Tory Grenville was a far cry from the glamour girl he'd imagined when he saw her photograph at Beva Scott's house two days earlier. He liked this incarnation better.

"Here. This is Tory," Beva had said, handing him a color proof sheet out of which several of the small images had been cut. One of Jolene, he knew, was taped to Amanda's mirror at home. Jolene probably had a shot of her best friend in a similar location.

The photograph Beva pointed out had been tiny, but not so small that Russ couldn't see he was looking at one gorgeous woman. Chestnut-brown hair tumbled to her shoulders. Unusual, almond-shaped hazel eyes stared at him. A small, secretive smile curved her lips.

A looker, he'd thought glumly. A pretty woman from away. He didn't want anything to do with another one of those. Melody had taught him how much unpleasantness could lurk beneath surface beauty.

She'd breezed into his life on a skiing vacation and turned his world upside down. For years he'd managed to convince himself they had the perfect marriage. Then she'd informed him that she had to get away before he bored her to death.

He'd barely had time to absorb the fact that she'd left him and their daughter before word came of the car crash that really had killed her.

Beva had denied she was playing matchmaker, but she'd remarked that the two of them, Russ and Tory, would look pretty darned good together.

Everyone had always said what a handsome couple he and Melody made. Russ knew now that outward appearance gave no clue to the person beneath. He'd take substance over surface beauty every time.

He'd felt nothing but relief when Tory Grenville first opened her door. This, he'd thought, was a woman he could talk to.

Oh, she was still the person whose photo he'd seen on the proof sheet. The eyes were a dead giveaway. But without all the cosmetics and the big hair, Tory was . . . approachable. Normal. Appealing. In person, she was animated in a way no still portrait could ever be.

Taking her invitation seriously, he continued

o look his fill, admiring the way she added just
he right amount of female pulchritude to her
oose, comfortable clothing. She was a tall woman.
He'd noticed that when she stood next to him in
he doorway. The top of her head had been level
with his shoulder, and he was six-foot-four.

As they had from the first, Tory's almond-
shaped eyes intrigued him. A puzzling sense of
amiliarity afflicted Russ as he gazed again into
heir hazel depths. He experienced the sudden,
strong feeling that he'd seen this woman before, a
ong time ago, but he could not place where or
when.

"You can stop staring now," she drawled.

"Sorry."

But he wasn't, except for the fact that his in-
ense scrutiny was having a predictable effect on
his body, one he hoped she wouldn't notice. He
didn't want her to realize how strongly he re-
ponded to everything about her. It wasn't just
what he was seeing. Her voice got to him too.
Sweet and melodic, with a lower register that was
undeniably sexy. And her scent. Something . . .
earthy.

Blinking rapidly, he fought a smile. It was
earthy, all right. She'd been in the garden. That
appealing smell was a mixture of sun-warmed soil
and feminine sweat and sunblock. The combination was astonishingly erotic.

"I think you have the wrong impression of
what I'm asking of you," he said. "Beva's the one

who thinks you should advise my daughter. What I want is someone to help me talk Amanda out of entering the pageant in the first place."

Even Tory's frown appealed to him. Russ had to remind himself again that he was not looking for a relationship. In the past couple of years he'd had to contend with more than one matchmaking effort. He'd been justifiably suspicious of Beva's insistence that only her friend could help him with Amanda.

"Relax," she'd told him, correctly interpreting the wary expression on his face. "Tory Grenville isn't any more interested in dating than you are. She went through a miserable divorce not very long ago. But she *is* the one who set up the photo session. She asked me to go with her for company and I decided to take Jolene, and then Jolene wanted to invite her best friend. . . ." Beva's voice had trailed off as she made a rotating gesture in the air. He'd gotten the picture.

"I don't know any Tory Grenville," he'd said, though he did know the old MacDougall place, where Beva told him Tory had been living since early summer.

Waycross Springs wasn't that big a town. Russ had gone to school with the MacDougalls' daughter. Mr. MacDougall, he recalled, had recently retired and left Maine for Arizona. He hadn't heard if the MacDougalls had sold their home or were only renting it. Neither did he know know what had happened to— What was her name? Oh, yes.

Vicki. He had equal difficulty calling up a memory of what she'd looked like. She'd been quiet. And a brain. No one had paid much attention to her. She'd left town after high school, and if she'd ever been back, he hadn't been told about it.

"You're looking at a desperate man," he said aloud when he realized both he and Tory had been silent for a couple of minutes. "Somehow, I have to convince Amanda that this competition is a bad idea."

"I can't imagine why you think I'd have any influence with her. We met only once and barely spoke." Tory had moved to stand by a window and now turned her back on him to stare out at her side lawn.

It was a very nice back, he thought, and an even nicer—

Russ curtailed his lascivious musings, grimacing at his lack of control. His libido was getting out of hand. Maybe coming there had been a mistake in more ways than one. Clearly she wasn't comfortable with the idea of talking to Amanda.

Time to cut his losses, Russ decided. He rose, ready to make excuses and leave, but just at that moment she spoke. Her words were so soft that he wasn't sure he'd heard her correctly.

"What?"

She turned. "I said I'll speak to her. Perhaps Amanda did get the wrong idea from that photo shoot. At the least I can make sure she understands why I had my picture taken."

"I really appreciate this. I mean, as you said, you barely know Amanda. You don't know me at all. I—" Something in her expression made him break off. "Do you?"

"There's no reason why you should remember me, Russ, but we did go to school together. All twelve years. Tory is short for Victoria. I went by Vicki when I was growing up here in Waycross Springs."

Floored, he simply stared at her for a long moment. *This* was Vicki MacDougall? Then, without thinking, he blurted out the first thing that came to mind. "You've changed some since then."

The Vicki he remembered had been skinny as a beanpole. She'd worn Coke-bottle glasses, which explained why he hadn't made the proper connection with her unusually shaped eyes. Vicki had been cursed with braces for several years too.

To his relief she laughed at his less-than-flattering remark. "That's an understatement if there ever was one."

"Is this the real you?" he asked, then winced as he realized he'd put his foot in his mouth again. "What I mean is that I saw the proof sheet with one of the pictures you had taken. You're apparently at least three different people. Young Vicki. Miss Glamour. And—" He gestured toward her, the woman he hoped was the real Tory Grenville. He definitely liked the version standing in front of him best of the three.

She shrugged. "The company I work for insisted I provide a photograph for the wall at corporate headquarters, and I decided I might as well have a little fun complying with the order."

"You sent them the photo I saw?" He tried to imagine a boss's reaction to the sexy, glamorous Tory Grenville.

"The pose they got was demure and serious, I assure you, though I must admit that I don't normally wear a lot of makeup or have my hair poufed up like that on the job."

He was curious about what she did for a living, but he hadn't come there to chitchat. And he had to return to the store soon. Get back to the purpose of this visit, he ordered himself. Don't let yourself be distracted by feminine charms.

"About Amanda. Vicki, I—"

"Tory. I left Vicki behind a long time ago."

"Tory, then."

It wasn't difficult to think of her by a different name. He'd never really known her when she was called Vicki. He wondered now if he'd missed something. She'd certainly grown into an interesting woman.

Stick to the subject at hand!

"My daughter returned from that photo shoot with stars in her eyes," he said. "Then this pageant came along as a direct result of the pictures she had taken. Because you were so involved in the first, I think she'll listen to you about the second. I'd really appreciate it if you'd help me talk her out of competing."

"Want some advice?" she asked after a moment.

"Sure." He'd listen. That didn't mean he had to go along with what she suggested.

"Let her do what she wants," Tory said. "Let Amanda enter the pageant."

"Not a chance."

"Isn't that kind of a hard line? It could backfire, given the way teenagers are."

"She's not a teenager yet!"

"Close enough. Anyway, for what it's worth, my advice is to lighten up."

"Only if you're volunteering to help," he muttered. "Not that I'm anywhere near ready to give in and allow her to enter," he added hastily, "but if I did agree to sign the permission slip, she'd have to have a chaperon." A small, rueful smile tugged at the corners of his mouth. "Somehow I can't see myself backstage trying to help her into a fancy dress or fixing her hair."

"Neither can I," Tory admitted. "But I can't visualize myself in that role either." With a sigh, she capitulated. "Guess we'd better talk her out of it. When would you like me to meet with her?"

"Tomorrow?"

"Tomorrow it is."

They set a time and place, and Russ thanked her and left. It was not until he was halfway back to the store that he allowed himself to analyze what had just happened. Although he'd been relieved when Tory said she'd help him convince

Amanda not to enter, he'd also had another, quite separate reaction.

Reluctantly, he reexamined the moment when she'd agreed. The sensation he'd felt was one he'd half forgotten, so long had it been since he'd experienced it, but he readily identified it now. In that instant he'd felt just like a teenager who'd finally gotten the girl he really, really liked to say she'd go out with him.

Don't think about the father, Tory warned herself. It's the daughter you're here to see.

A little more than twenty-four hours after Russ Tandy had appeared on her doorstep, on a bright and sunny Sunday afternoon, Tory stood on the Tandys' front porch. There was no sign of a bell, so she used the brass knocker, a figure of a man playing the bagpipes.

She had to chuckle at that. Not only had the Tandy family owned the local music store when she was growing up, but Russ's father had kicked off a lively debate on noise pollution when one of his neighbors had objected to him practicing his piping in his yard. She didn't think she'd ever heard him on the pipes, but she knew he'd been able to play most of the instruments he sold. Tandy's Music and Gifts used to offer five free lessons to the children of parents who purchased any item in stock. Except for the piano, she remembered. In Waycross Springs, that instruction had been and probably still was Hildegarde Benning's exclusive domain.

Russ's house was the same one he'd grown up in, an old Victorian painted white with green trim and sporting a wide, balustraded porch with room for lots of summer furniture. Just like her parents, Russ's mother and father had passed the old homestead on to the next generation and moved to a warmer climate. According to Beva, the senior Tandys had done so nearly ten years earlier, about the same time the Scotts moved to Waycross Springs. Russ's father had been a lot older than her own, Tory recalled, and compared with most folks around there, her dad had started his family late.

Tory knew the exterior of the Tandy house very well. More than once she'd deliberately taken a detour past it on her way home from school, even though it was out of her way.

A rueful smile tugged at her mouth. What a loser she'd been, mooning over the big sports star, too shy to say boo to a goose, let alone a boy. No wonder Russ hadn't recognized her.

The door opened abruptly, cutting off bittersweet reminiscences. The girl Tory remembered from their trip to the photography studio stood before her, a sullen expression on her pretty face. The pursed lips, narrowed eyes, and belligerent stance warned Tory that Amanda might resent her interference.

There was no sign of Russ, but Tory suspected

he wasn't far off. Sunday was the only day of the week his store was closed. She felt sure he customarily spent it with his daughter. But how much had he told Amanda about Tory's visit? Tory doubted he'd revealed that she intended to try to discourage Amanda from entering the pageant.

"I know why you're here," the girl said.

"Oh, you do, do you?" Tory fought the urge to wipe suddenly sweaty palms on the sides of her gray wool slacks.

Russ's daughter didn't move aside to let her enter the house, nor did she speak again. She stared at Tory, daring her to make her first move.

Determined no twelve-year-old would get the better of her in the first round, Tory plunked herself down on an old-fashioned porch glider and assumed the demeanor of someone who couldn't care less what Amanda Tandy thought. Using one foot, she set the wooden glider in motion.

"Aren't you going to try to talk me out of competing?" A tiny note of doubt had crept into the girl's voice.

"Where did you get the idea that I was?"

"The look on Daddy's face when he said you'd be stopping by."

Tory would have given a great deal to know exactly what expression that had been. Smug, perhaps? She could hardly ask.

The door closed, but not to shut Tory out. A few steps and Amanda stood in front of the glider, studying its occupant with blatant curiosity. Her arms were crossed protectively in front of her chest, but nothing else gave away any uncertainty.

Tory kept her gaze locked on Amanda's, hoping the girl would not suddenly decide to retreat. Russ had raised a self-confident, articulate child, a far cry from the girl Tory had been.

"Maybe I'm just planning to use you to get in good with your father," Tory said. She regretted the outrageous statement immediately. It was far too possible, unsettlingly so, that her hasty words contained a smidgen of truth.

Was that the real reason she'd agreed to this? To see if, after all these years, shy little Vicki might have a chance with the high-school hero?

That conclusion made as much sense as any other reason she'd been able to come up with. She hadn't known what possessed her when she'd agreed to help Russ. The words had seemed to pop out all by themselves when she'd heard sounds behind her to suggest he was preparing to leave her living room . . . her home . . . her life.

Disgusted with herself, Tory was about to issue a retraction when Amanda forestalled her. "If you want to catch him for a husband," the girl said, "you'll have to convince Daddy to let me enter the pageant."

"How do you figure that?" Tory felt genuinely curious. "You obviously know he's not in favor of it." She caught herself toying with the edge of one blue silk cuff and stilled her fingers before Amanda noticed.

"Simple. If you help me, then you'll have an excuse to spend a lot of time here. And I'll go to bed really, really early, so you'll have plenty of chances to"—she paused, searching for the right words—"work your wiles on him."

Wiles? "Amanda, I—"

"No, this will work. This is good." Amanda dropped to the floor of the porch and wrapped her arms around her upraised knees, resting her chin on her folded hands so she could continue to stare at Tory.

"Amanda, you'd better think about this." Tory heard her voice rise as a ribbon of panic wound through her. This conversation was not going the way she'd planned. Not at all.

"It's okay. I always knew Daddy had to start dating sometime. Jolene and I thought you'd be okay the first time we met you, when we all had our pictures taken."

Faced with Russ's daughter, boldly declaring that she was the chosen one, momentarily left Tory at a loss for words.

Those crucial seconds of hesitation cost her any chance of completing her mission. Amanda was well launched into a list of the things they'd have to do to prepare for the pageant before Tory could draw breath to protest. The Miss Special Smile agenda rivaled the practice schedule of a professional sports team.

Holding both hands up in the sign for time-out, Tory brought the glider to a shuddering halt. Amanda stopped speaking, but her dark eyes, eyes very like her father's, remained alight with enthusiasm.

"Let me get this straight," Tory said. "You've been sizing up potential girlfriends for your father?"

Amanda loosed her grip on her knees enough to enable her to gesture with both hands. "Hey, who can do it better? And it's obvious by now that he's not going to go out and find someone on his own."

He wouldn't have to, Tory thought. Women would flock to him at the crook of his little finger.

"You don't know anything about me," she protested aloud. "I could be a terrible person. The most wicked of potential wicked stepmothers."

"Nah. Mrs. Scott likes you. You must be okay."

This was way too tempting, Tory thought. She ought to leave. Now. Before Russ himself came out of the house and vanquished all her good intentions with his killer smile.

"We have to get moving," Amanda said earnestly. "The deadline for sending in the application is less than a week away."

"Why?" Tory asked, hating how weak her own voice sounded.

She didn't seem to be leaving.

No willpower.

How absurd!

"Why what?" Amanda asked.

"Why do you want to compete?" That seemed the safer subject. With a silent groan, Tory realized she'd just tacitly agreed to back Amanda's entry into the pageant.

The girl rattled off a list of benefits that sounded as if she'd memorized them from pageant literature. "Participants gain self-confidence," she repeated at the end. "I think that's very important. Don't you?"

"I think that's something you already have in plentiful supply."

"I'll get scholarship money when I win. Daddy says there's never enough of that."

"What if you don't win?" Tory countered.

Amanda came over to the glider and squeezed in at Tory's side, gazing up at her beseechingly. "Didn't you ever want something so bad you could taste it? I have to try. I just have to."

"And if you don't win?" Tory repeated. She took Amanda's hands in her own. She knew a lot more about losing than she did about winning, but that was a life experience she'd just as soon not share with Russ's child.

"Daddy says I'm resilient," Amanda declared. "I'll bounce back."

"Are you sure you're only twelve?"

Amanda nodded vigorously. "You will help me, won't you?"

Capitulating with a sigh, just as she had the

previous day under pressure from this child's father, Tory agreed to help. "But it's not to get in good with your dad," she insisted. "I just said I was interested in him to rile you."

At once she was captured in an exuberant hug. "I knew that." Amanda's whisper was followed by a giggle. "But it's okay if you change your mind. You'd make a cool stepmom."

Late the same afternoon, Russ tracked Tory down. He located her in her backyard, seated on a swing hung from a high branch of an old elm tree at the corner of the property.

"I've been banging on your front door for at least ten minutes," he informed her. He was not in a good mood. Tory had betrayed him. She'd done just the opposite of what he'd asked.

"I make no excuses for what I've done," she responded. "I agreed to help Amanda through the pageant." Her chin rose to a defiant angle as she glared at him.

"You were supposed to talk her out of it," he said when he was close enough to glower effectively.

"I agreed to try!"

Clearly she did not intend to apologize. His attitude was only provoking her ire.

"Your daughter really wants to enter the pageant, Russ. She's willing to work hard toward that goal. I don't think it's going to hurt her any to take on the responsibility. My only real concern is how she'll handle losing, but even then she should learn something valuable from the experience."

"Amanda has been in competitions before. She can deal with defeat. But in this case, she won't have to. She's not going to win or lose because she's not going to enter. You need to talk to her again. Tomorrow, after school. You and Jolene both. At Beva's house. Between you, surely the two of you can—"

"By the time school gets out tomorrow," Tory informed him, "I'll be on my way to Ireland."

"You're going on a vacation? Now?" Thunderstruck, he moved a few steps closer to the swing. To avoid him, she balanced on her toes and edged herself to one side.

"It's a business trip. In case you've forgotten, I do work for a living."

He'd been trying not to remember anything at all about her. He hadn't had much success banishing her from his consciousness. His decision not to see her when she called on his daughter had definitely backfired. After Tory left, Amanda had gleefully informed him that she was all set . . . she had a chaperon. The only thing she still needed was his signature on the permission slip.

"I'll be home again at the end of the week," Tory said. "While I'm gone, Amanda can send in her application. There may even be time for her to receive her acceptance."

Lifting her legs, Tory swung toward him. He

barely had time to step out of the way and avoid a collision.

Unrepentant, Tory leaned back as far as she could without releasing the ropes. Her toes pointed toward the sky.

Russ abruptly lost his train of thought. He couldn't focus on anything but the luxuriant chestnut tresses trailing almost to the ground. The sun glinted off her hair, blinding him to anything else. He found himself wondering how a lock of it would feel against his fingers. Masses of it trailing over his bare chest. Brushing lower.

Dragging his gaze away from her hair, he focused on her profile, then her silhouette, his gaze skimming over her as she seemed to arch upward just for his inspection.

She'd traded the previous day's grubbies for tailored slacks and a pale blue silk blouse. Her movement on the swing molded the thin fabric to the curve of her throat, the rise of her breasts.

Blinking rapidly, he tried to force his mind back to the matter at hand. This woman wasn't interested in him. He wasn't even sure she was all that concerned about his daughter.

His voice gruff, he demanded, "Are you going to be Amanda's chaperon or not?"

With a graceful movement she came upright again. She met his eyes. "Yes."

"If you're going to be gone all the time, how can you—"

"My schedule is pretty clear for the next couple of months. Just this one quick trip to Ireland and another to company headquarters in Houston." She shrugged, as if all that flying from place to place was nothing out of the ordinary.

Russ wondered what she'd think of him if he told her he'd never once traveled by air.

"Don't worry, Russ. I can arrange to spend plenty of time with Amanda. Since there's no talking her out of the pageant, isn't it better to agree to let me help?"

"I don't want her to enter."

And if he consented, he thought, both he and Amanda would be spending a lot of time with Tory Grenville. Not a great idea. She'd crept into his mind far too often during the last twenty-four hours as it was. He hadn't been visualizing her as Amanda's chaperon, either. In increasingly erotic daydreams, he'd seen her as a much more intimate type of companion—for himself.

"You're just being stubborn," Tory told him. "There was no harm in the trip to the photographer's and I doubt there's any in this pageant." Pushing with both feet, she launched the swing into motion. The rush of air caught her loose hair, tumbling it about her face.

"My instincts say I should forbid it. Refuse to sign that permission slip." His instincts said a few other things as he watched her fly higher, but he struggled to ignore them.

After a bit she grounded the swing again and began to spin idly in a circle, twisting the ropes

above her head. "Deny her and you'll only succeed in making yourself into the bad guy."

"Don't push me, Tory. I know what's best for
my own child."

She looked up at him with bewitching hazel
eyes, then let the swing unwind in a rush that had
him reaching for her, afraid she'd tumble onto the
ground and hurt herself.

"Why don't you push back?" she invited in a
husky whisper when he caught the ropes on either
side of her head and suddenly found himself face-
to-face with her. Her lips were only inches from
his mouth.

Abruptly he straightened. He knew he should
walk away. Instead, he stepped behind her and
grasped the back of the rough wooden seat. His
thumbs grazed her bottom.

A rhythm quickly established itself. He
pushed. She pumped her legs. On each backswing,
his fingers brushed against her. The contact was
slight, but he felt a distinct tingle every time they
connected.

The swing went higher and higher, and as she
soared, his spirits lifted. Maybe he *was* being stubborn, Russ thought. Too stubborn for his own
good.

Tory was apparently agreeable to spending
time with his daughter, and he could no longer
deny that he wanted to spend time with Tory. Not
to himself, anyway.

"Okay," he said, pushing again.

"Okay what?" She sounded breathless as she flew away from him.

"You're right." Another push. "I know when I'm licked. Amanda alone would probably have worn me down. With your support, my defeat became inevitable."

As if by silent agreement, they let the swing slow, then stop. He held on to the thick, prickly ropes at the level of her shoulders.

"So what do we do now?" he asked. It seemed wisest to keep talking about his daughter.

"Nothing for the moment. After you sign the permission slip, it's her responsibility to send in the application and start looking for financial backers."

"I can give her the money." She started to object, but he talked over her words. "Tandy Music and Gifts is a legitimate sponsor."

"Of course it is, but the experience of talking to other store owners will be good for her. Trust me. I'm in sales. It's a useful skill to learn."

He slowly walked around the swing, facing her but keeping hold of the ropes. "How come you're living here if your company's in Texas?"

"In sales, we travel a lot. Since I can do the rest of my work from a home office, I can live anywhere I choose."

"And you chose here? In the back of beyond?" He knew he sounded skeptical, but most people who left town after high school did not return for more than brief visits.

She shrugged and stared at the circle she was inscribing on the ground with the toe of one shoe. "When my folks started talking about selling their house, the house I grew up in, I started remembering the good things about small-town life. I offered to buy it. I thought I had cut all my ties with the past, but it bothered me to think there would be no place for me here once they moved away." Once again she lifted one shoulder, a seemingly negligent gesture. "I guess there's just something appealing about a place like Waycross Springs. And it's . . . home."

A home where she could hardly know anyone anymore, Russ mused. And just when all her family were leaving. That didn't add up until he remembered she'd only recently been divorced. Traumatic life experiences did have a tendency to make people want to go back to their roots.

What kind of fool, he wondered, would let a woman like this one go?

She stood without warning, forcing him to release the ropes and back away quickly or risk a collision between the top of her head and the underside of his jaw. "Tell Amanda that we'll go clothes shopping next weekend. And start to experiment with makeup. And tell her she needs to decide what to do for the talent competition. I assume she's as musical as the rest of the Tandys."

"Yes," he said, answering the question first, but the talent portion of the pageant was not what concerned him. "I won't have her turned into a dressed-up doll."

"Trust me, Russ. Okay?"

At his reluctant nod, she headed back toward her house. He followed her brisk strides at a slower pace. "She's growing up too fast already," he muttered under his breath.

Everything in his life seemed to be moving too fast for comfort.

THREE

Tory pretended not to hear Russ's grumbling.

"I help with what I know," she said, glancing back at him. "You help with what you know."

What she knew, Tory thought, was that she was entirely too attracted to Russ Tandy. Back there on the swing, she'd started having all kinds of absurd fantasies. And before that, fool that she was, she'd actually been flirting with him.

Probably the fault of the way he was dressed, she told herself. For the first time since they were teenagers, she was seeing him in jeans. Snug, faded jeans with the stress points defined by blue denim faded to nearly white by long wear and frequent washings. If he'd been appealing in the comfortable dress slacks he'd worn the day before, he was breathtaking in fabric that hugged his thighs and also called attention to buns to die for.

The zippered sweatshirt that went with the

jeans should have looked baggy, even sloppy. Not on Russ. With the sleeves pushed up, it just emphasized the perfection of his arms and shoulders. Tory sighed. No man should be allowed to look that good in old clothes. One glance had sent her hormones into a spin, making her intensely aware of certain parts of her own anatomy. All that was distinctly female in her body, areas to which she rarely paid any mind, were suddenly clamoring for some male attention.

Shape up, she told herself sternly. Hadn't she learned anything during her marriage? That had been one long disappointment, both emotionally and physically. She'd come away from it wondering how any couple stayed together. As for sex— she did not understand what all the fuss was about. She doubted she'd ever marry again, and sex without marriage, which at least provided practical things like family health insurance and joint mortgages, hardly seemed worthwhile.

And yet, something strange happened every time she was in the vicinity of Russ Tandy. She couldn't figure it out. She was a little old to still have a crush on him, but the physical symptoms, and the way he lingered in her mind when he wasn't anywhere around, all pointed to the same unpalatable conclusion. She reverted to adolescence in his presence. She supposed she should be grateful she could still string words together and that she didn't blush every time he spoke to her.

It helped if she stayed irritated at him.

Unfortunately, he'd just caved in. Agreed to what Amanda wanted. What Tory herself had asked for. She was torn between being pleased their campaign had succeeded and very, very worried about what the future held.

"Tory?"

From the puzzled expression on his face, this was not the first time he'd spoken her name. She'd reached the top step of the short flight of stairs leading to her side porch. Russ stood just below her, which brought their eyes level.

"I'm sorry. A lot on my mind. What did you say?"

"I asked what I know." He shook his head at her obvious incomprehension and tried again. "You said you'd help with what you know and that I should help with what I know. What do I know about beauty pageants?"

What did *she* know? Tory wondered. Not a heck of a lot. She forced her disquiet aside and attempted to answer him. "I hope you know what to do about Amanda's talent competition. I hate to confess this, but I have a tin ear. No musical ability whatsoever. So if your daughter can play some instrument or sing, then you're the—"

"Bagpipes," he said.

"Excuse me?"

"Bagpipes. Amanda plays the bagpipes. So do I. I've been competing for years, as my father did before me and still does. As my brother Gordon does, when he can. It's by way of being a family tradition."

"Good grief." Why did it have to be bagpipes? The instrument made a sound like a cat being strangled. Tory had always thought it grated on the nerves worse than fingernails on a chalkboard.

"What? You don't respond to the skirling of the pipes? And you a MacDougall!"

"A Scottish surname doesn't mean I have to love everything associated with that heritage. I've never developed a taste for haggis, either. I don't mean to insult you, but the thought of anyone piping, even Amanda, does not thrill me."

"Don't worry about it. Most people have strong reactions to the pipes. Love them or hate them. It's rare for someone to feel ambivalent."

"Maybe Amanda will select a quieter instrument to play. She must have learned others."

"Of course she did. But she'll pick the pipes." A faraway look came into Russ's eyes, fascinating Tory. "Teaching her has been one of the great joys of my life the last few years. Amanda and I go out into the country so we won't disturb the neighbors and march up and down, side by side, scaring the crows and sending the woodchucks scurrying into the safety of their holes."

When she started thinking she'd like to see that, especially if Russ wore a kilt, Tory knew it was time for him to be on his way.

"You and Amanda talk about the talent portion of the program. I'll be back on Friday. Give me a chance to readjust to the time change and then I'll be ready to take her shopping."

Sometime Saturday afternoon, she thought. When she was rested.

And when Russ was safely at work at the store.

While she was away, she hoped she'd be able to analyze her unprecedented reaction to Russ Tandy. Or, even better, keep so busy she wouldn't have time to give him a single thought. Yes, she decided. It would be best if she simply forgot all about him. Ignored his existence and the peculiar effect he had on her.

"Okay," he said, and stuck out his hand. Doubts still lurked in his eyes, but since he seemed to want to shake on their agreement, Tory could hardly refuse without seeming churlish. She executed a firm, businesslike clasp and quick release.

Even that brief touch made her blood sing in her veins. As soon as he broke contact and said he had to be going, she turned away from him, fumbling at the catch on the door, wanting nothing more than to retreat behind the illusory safety of mesh screening.

Fortunately, Russ didn't seem aware of her reaction. As she watched him walk away, however, Tory had the oddest sensation that she was still on the swing, twirling in meaningless circles, moving back and forth between relief and disappointment.

⬥―――⬥

Gordon Tandy wore the uniform of the Way-cross Springs Police Department. By rights, he should have been in the music business, just like Russ, but there was a rebel in every generation. Their uncle had joined the marines and ended up living in Hawaii. Granddad's brother had gone to Alaska. The generations before that had produced explorers, pioneers, and adventurers, who had reached places as far-flung as Tahiti and Leadville, Colorado. Russ supposed he should be grateful Gordon had at least stayed close to home.

His profession had its uses as well. The two brothers were meeting over coffee at Glendorra's, which featured Maxwell House and Folgers and pretended never to have heard the words *espresso* or *cappuccino*, to discuss the results of the query Gordon had put on a cops-only police digest on the Internet.

"The official records show arrests and convictions," Gordon said, "but these guys share the good stuff."

"And?" Russ took a long swig from an oversize mug. Not as good as the coffee Beva brewed, he thought.

"The pageant looks clean. No scandals. No charges of misconduct on anybody's part, and no rigging the results, either. Well, we should have figured that, I guess. You know the folks at the Sinclair House. They wouldn't allow an event to be held on their premises if there was anything shady about it."

Russ did know Lucas Sinclair. The hotel manager was only two years his senior. They'd been students at the local high school at the same time, played on the same basketball team. Lucas was as honest as the day was long.

But Russ also knew the hotel had experienced some financial problems over the last few years. And he didn't know much about the new person in charge of special events and public relations, the woman he'd talked to on the phone last week—except that she'd married Lucas the previous May.

"It would have been nice to find a solid excuse to yank Amanda out of the competition," Russ grumbled.

"Sorry, bro. Besides, you know what a softy you are with your kid. You never deny her anything she really wants."

"She's never wanted anything so outrageous before."

Gordon gave him an odd look over the rim of his mug. "She got you to buy her that dog, didn't she?"

Russ had forgotten the dog. A miniature poodle. Amanda had begged and pleaded and he'd given in, even though it was obvious the blasted creature had been born with the temperament of a pit bull. To make things worse, the woman he'd employed back then to clean the house, a job he and Amanda did nowadays, had turned out to be allergic to dog dander and quit on them. Fortunately, Amanda had soon realized for herself that the pup wasn't working out. Probably after it nipped her for the second or third time. She'd dealt with the problem by finding it a new home with someone who had a way with canines, even psychotic ones.

"Amanda handled that mess very well," Russ said proudly, "and she was only nine at the time."

"So maybe she can handle this on her own too."

"I got her some help. Remember Victoria MacDougall? She was in my class in school." Gordon was three years Russ's junior and took a lot of kidding because he had the kind of boyish good looks that made him appear even younger. He had the same wavy hair and brown eyes Russ did, but Gordon was shorter and bulkier, and his facial features were less sharply defined.

"Vicki MacDougall? Sure, I remember her. She came back to town a few months ago, when her folks moved south. I ran into her a couple of weeks back. She was having a drink in the bar at the Phoenix with Roger Hillary."

Russ wasn't sure which surprised him more, that Tory had been keeping company with someone like Hillary or that they'd met at the Phoenix Inn, one of the most disreputable establishments in Waycross Springs. Had he made a mistake by entrusting his daughter to Tory's care? Had he been off base in his own judgment of the woman?

"So?" Gordon prompted him. "How does

Vicki MacDougall fit into this beauty-pageant business? I mean, she turned out okay in the looks department, but she's no glamour girl."

"Tory," Russ corrected him. "She goes by Tory now and the last name is Grenville. She's divorced. Beva Scott recommended I ask her to help Amanda with the pageant."

Gordon gave a nod, as if that explained everything, and drained his mug. "Got to get back to work," he said. "Anything else I can answer for you, bro?"

Russ resisted the temptation to share with his brother his confused feelings about Tory. It seemed too soon to confide in anyone, even Gordon, just how much he missed her. It had barely been three days since he'd last seen her and he could hardly wait until she returned.

Still, there was one thing he did have to ask. "That night you saw them. Did Roger and Tory seem . . . close?"

Roger Hillary had been one of the nerds. As "Vicki" had been, Russ recalled with a grimace. But unlike her, good old Rog had stayed in Waycross Springs and found an outlet for his weirdness by running an electronics store that also sold computer games and rented videos. He'd built a none too savory reputation as a purveyor of X-rated material to the less desirable element among the tourists.

"More like old friends getting together for a drink," Gordon told him. "I doubt she knows much about what he's doing these days." He waited, giving Russ ample opportunity to say more.

Russ waved him off. They'd agreed long ago that it was better not to inquire too closely into each other's relationships with the fair sex. Years earlier Gordon had tried to warn Russ about Melody . . . and gotten himself punched in the nose for his trouble.

As he watched the other man leave the coffee shop, Russ hoped Gordon was right about Tory, that she was ignorant of Roger Hillary's business practices. Trouble was, he didn't really know much about her. Only what he'd seen. What she'd told him.

What he'd felt in her presence.

He shook his head, trying to clear his thoughts. She'd grown up to be a vibrant, appealing woman. Belatedly, he realized what he'd been feeling ever since Gordon mentioned Tory and Roger in the same breath.

He was jealous.

Somehow, between their second meeting at her place and now, he'd started to feel possessive. He didn't just want her help with Amanda. He wanted to monopolize the rest of her time himself.

Bad idea. Much smarter to put as much emotional and physical distance between them as possible.

He walked back to the shop, which had been

left in the hands of his one part-time employee, Maud Ruthven, a widow who supplemented her retirement income by helping him out ten hours a week, and found a message slip waiting for him.

So much for his plan to avoid Tory, he thought. It looked like he'd be seeing a lot more of her.

The pageant coordinators had moved fast. Amanda had mailed her application and the permission slip in first thing Monday morning. It had been received that day and acted upon immediately. In the phone call he'd missed to take the coffee break with his brother, Amanda had been accepted as a contestant in the Miss Special Smile competition, provided she showed sufficient poise during the personal-interview phase of the process.

"Friday?" he muttered in disbelief, staring at the message slip in his hand.

"The woman on the phone said you lucked out," Maud told him, her faded blue eyes bright with curiosity. She was a tiny woman, all skin and bones, but she had the energy of a teenager. Except when her knees bothered her—always a sign of bad weather to come—she was in perpetual motion, darting here and there to dust shelves and rearrange stock, hands fluttering as she chattered happily with any customers who came in to browse or buy.

Briefly, Russ explained about the pageant.

"How did I luck out?" he asked when he'd hit all the highlights.

"Well," said Maud. "It just so happens that the pageant coordinators are scheduled to be at the Sinclair House on Friday, to check out the facilities. That's why they can talk to Amanda at three that afternoon."

"How considerate." Eager for their four hundred bucks, no doubt.

"It really is," Maud insisted. "The woman explained it to me. Seems that if you can't make it Friday, you'll have to take Amanda to Portland for her interview. Stand in line with hundreds of other parents and kids."

That thought was enough to make him shudder.

"She also said that although parents are not permitted to sit in on the interview, you can meet at the same hour with a Ms. Arsenica to ask questions."

Birdlike, Maud hovered, waiting to see what crumb he would drop next.

Russ reached for the phone. He had questions all right. And just to make sure he thought of everything he should ask, he wanted Tory with him. She'd said she'd be home Friday. Increasingly uncomfortable under Maud's scrutiny, he left a succinct message on Tory's answering machine, suggesting she meet him at the Sinclair House on that day at three on the dot.

———◆———

The Sinclair House was as posh as ever, Tory thought as she entered the old-fashioned lobby through a door held open by a uniformed employee. She remembered how much she'd loved coming to this hotel as a child. Each Christmas Eve, the Sinclairs threw a big party and invited everyone in town. She'd been to one or two other events over the years too. Lenny Goldman's bar mitzvah. Delia Conway's wedding reception.

Don't dawdle.

She could look around and reminisce later. Right now Russ was waiting for her.

She fought down a prickle of anticipation. This wasn't about Tory and Russ, she warned herself. They were getting together only because of Amanda.

Wishing she'd had time to take a nap after returning from her trip, Tory followed the directions given to her at the front desk and climbed to the second floor of the hotel. Jet-lagged and with the makings of a fine headache, she'd been back in Waycross Springs all of an hour. She'd found Russ's message waiting on her voice mail.

For a moment after listening to it, she'd been annoyed. He'd sounded as if he was giving an order rather than making a request. Rationalization had followed quickly. He was not a man who liked asking favors. And he probably didn't care much for answering machines either.

There had been no question but that she would meet him, which had sent her into a brief panic. She hadn't planned to see Russ again until she was rested, strong enough to deal with the powerful emotions he aroused in her every time they got within shouting distance.

A switch to her business persona had been all that saved her from crumbling then and there. She'd made a mental list and followed it to the letter, even though she knew doing so would make her a trifle late. She'd fed the cats, taken a quick shower, and dressed in the one business suit she hadn't taken with her, a conservative navy-blue skirt and matching jacket. A short drive had brought her to the hotel, her head clearer and her brain more or less functional. If she was lucky, she thought as she hurried along the deeply carpeted hallway, she wouldn't fade until this meeting was over.

She had no idea what to expect as she rapped lightly on the third door to her right. It was now ten minutes past three. Russ would already have arrived. Her heart rate accelerated at the thought of being with him again.

A woman Tory had never seen before opened the door and invited her in. She was smiling pleasantly, but all Tory saw, looking past her, was Russ's scowl. He stood by the window, impatience radiating from every pore.

"I'm Gayla Arsenica," the woman said, holding out a hand.

Tory took it. "Nice to meet you. I'm Victoria—"

"You're late," Russ interrupted.

Both women turned to stare at him, surprised by his rudeness.

Tory's reaction was automatic. She didn't stand for such treatment in the workplace and she wasn't about to put up with it here. "Will you excuse us, Ms. Arsenica? I need to speak to Russ for a moment. In the hall."

The pageant coordinator smiled graciously. Russ started to object, then apparently caught sight of Tory's implacable expression and thought better of it. He followed her lead meekly enough, but he closed the door behind them with a bit more force than necessary.

Tory's headache abruptly returned. Sheer weariness threatened to buckle her knees, but she refused to let any weakness show. "What's your problem, Russ?" she demanded in a heated whisper. "I'm here to do you a favor. Remember?"

"I remember that you got me into this!"

"Oh, no. Don't blame me." Her eyes narrowed. "Did Ms. Arsenica say something to rile you?"

They were nose to nose in the quiet corridor, carrying on an acrimonious discussion, almost a quarrel, in whispers. The absurdity of it hit Tory at the same moment it appeared to strike Russ. A sheepish expression crept over his face.

"Could we start over?" he asked, still whispering.

"Sure."

"Welcome home, Tory."

"Thank you. It's good to be back."

At her slow, tired smile, he broke eye contact to stare at his shoes. "I was out of line," he muttered. "I'll grovel properly later. Right now we need to finish this meeting. I have to get back to the store."

"What did I miss?"

"Ms. Arsenica was just telling me how pleased she was to have a local contestant. Amanda's the only one from these parts to enter." He glanced at his watch. "I have to leave within the next fifteen minutes. Could you—"

"I'll stay if there's more to ask. Where's Amanda?"

"In her interview. She's going to Jolene's when she's finished. Come to our place for dinner later?"

"And that groveling you promised?"

A fractional hesitation preceded his answer. "Yeah."

"I'll let you know."

They went back into the room. Russ at once began firing questions at the pageant coordinator. His skepticism was evident, but he was unfailingly polite, and Ms. Arsenica said all the right things in a voice designed to soothe and placate. After ten minutes Russ made his excuses and stood to shrug into his leather coat.

Ms. Arsenica beamed at both Tory and Russ. "I can see how, as Amanda's parents, you'd want to—" She broke off at the stricken expression on Russ's face, then looked quickly at Tory.

For a moment Tory was swamped with emotions. Sympathy for Russ mixed with unexpectedly strong feelings of hurt and rejection. His reaction told her more clearly than any words how he felt about being linked with her, even by mistake.

Forcing an amused smile to her lips, she addressed the pageant coordinator. "It's perfectly natural that you'd jump to the conclusion that we're both Amanda's parents, especially after what must have appeared to be a marital tiff out in the hall. Russ cut me off earlier before I could tell you my last name. It's Grenville. I'm just . . . a friend. I'm helping out."

"Amanda's mother died four years ago." Russ's voice was gruff. He'd already been leaving. Now he all but bolted for the door, mumbling the conventional phrases as he went.

Tory unclenched her fingers from the arm of her chair. Exhaustion and a sharp sense of disappointment, foolish as she knew that feeling to be, combined to rob her of energy. If she'd been alone, she'd have cursed. Or cried.

Instead she rallied, turning to face Ms. Arsenica once more. With any luck, the other woman hadn't guessed how deeply her casual assumption had affected both Russ and Tory.

She asked one or two questions about the clothes Amanda would need, then gathered up her lightweight coat. She'd just slipped into it when the phone rang. Ms. Arsenica signaled her to wait.

"Amanda came through her interview with flying colors," she announced a moment later.

"Thanks for telling me," Tory said. "And thank you for your time."

"I apologize again for my earlier mistake, but I must say that you two make a lovely couple."

For one brief moment Tory let herself imagine it—herself and Russ as Amanda's parents. As husband and wife. As lovers.

The vision was indescribably appealing.

Unfortunately, it took two to make that sort of dream come true, and half of this potential couple didn't seem to be interested.

All the way home from the hotel she gave herself yet another stern lecture. She'd spent most of her high-school years pining for a boy named Russ Tandy, dreaming impossible daydreams about the future they'd have together if he ever noticed she was alive. Well, now he'd noticed, but he wanted her for his daughter, not himself. And on a temporary basis, at that.

Russ Tandy the man was every bit as desirable to the woman she'd become as the boy had been to the girl, but Tory had learned a few things in the intervening years. She'd loved and lost and

had come to regret letting emotions rule her.
Never again would she allow herself blindly to
follow her heart. And never again would she waste
a single minute longing for what was out of her
reach.

She'd simply have to focus on Amanda and ignore Russ.

A sigh escaped her as she pulled into her ga-
rage. Easier said than done. She could get out of
dinner that night easily enough, but she had a
feeling that the next few weeks were going to
seem an eternity.

Tandy's Music and Gifts looked out across the
town park with its nineteenth-century bandstand
and monument to Civil War veterans. Russ spotted Tory and Amanda the moment they stepped
onto the leaf-strewn paths from the corner of
Park and Grove streets.

Fall had come a little late that year. There
were still plenty of bright leaves on the branches.
The color was just past peak here in western
Maine, or so the weathermen were saying. In New
Hampshire and southern Maine the trees had yet
to achieve their best color.

The tall, hazel-eyed, chestnut-haired woman
and the child with the golden hair and big brown
eyes fit right in with nature's decor.

As Russ watched Tory and Amanda laugh together and try to juggle too many shopping bags,

he could not help noticing the rapport between them. What existed between himself and Tory was harder to define.

The night before, he'd still been prepared to grovel, even though Ms. Arsenica's mistaken impression had bothered him more than he wanted to admit. He'd never gotten the chance. By the time he went to pick up his daughter, Tory had already called Amanda at Beva's to beg off dinner. She'd said she was about to crash, done in by jet lag, and had arranged to meet Amanda this afternoon for their shopping expedition. She'd left no private word for him.

Probably just as well, he thought as he turned away from the display window. Saved him having to admit that at least part of the reason for his bad temper the previous day had been fear for Tory's safety. How did a grown man explain that he did not trust airplanes? Or that because she'd been a few minutes late for their meeting, he'd gone into a blind panic?

There was no other word for it. He'd been sure she'd been in an accident, and the thought that he might never see her again had devastated him. The depth of his sense of loss had just sunk in when she'd turned up, completely unaware of what he'd been going through. For some inexplicable reason, her blithe, self-confident entrance had punched all the wrong buttons. He'd lashed out, angry at himself for caring too deeply, but taking out his bad temper on her.

Stupid.

Irrational.

What was it about Tory Grenville that made him act in ways that were totally out of character?

He wasn't entirely sure he wanted to know the answer to that question.

The bell above the door sounded, ending his uncomfortable bout of self-analysis. His whirlwind daughter came in first, strewing packages in her wake as she dashed the length of the store and threw herself into his arms.

"Daddy! I found the most gorgeous dress! It's way cool!"

He hugged her back, then ruffled her hair. "And you said you'd have to go all the way to the mall in south Portland to get something," he teased.

"Tory's great," Amanda declared, eyes shining. "She found it. I didn't even want to try it on. It didn't look like anything on the hanger. But it's perfect. Just perfect."

Over Amanda's head, Russ watched Tory gather up the scattered bags and deposit them, together with the ones she'd been carrying, behind the counter. She avoided meeting his eyes.

Uh-oh, he thought. Was she upset with him? Or was there something he wasn't going to like about this "perfect" dress? They were talking about an evening gown for a beauty pageant here, for the "formal wear" segment of the contest. A sinking feeling in his stomach, he set his daughter away from him.

"Want to model it for me?" he asked.

Eyes alight with pure pleasure, she made no verbal answer. Snatching up two of the bags as she went, Amanda was off again, through the door behind the counter and into his private office, which had its own rest room where she could change clothes.

He watched her go, figuring he now had five minutes, tops, alone with Tory. He intended to make good use of them.

FOUR

Tory felt Russ's gaze upon her, but she avoided looking his way. She was there to help Amanda, she reminded herself. If her heart rate had speeded up and her breathing got labored the moment she entered the store, surely that was only the result of a brisk walk across the park.

"This dress . . ." Russ let the words trail off, as if he was uncertain what he wanted to ask.

"Wait and see for yourself," she answered.

Even as she spoke Tory attempted to focus on her surroundings instead of on Amanda's father. It had been a long time since she'd been in Tandy's Music and Gifts. Years. A wide selection of CDs, audiocassettes, and gift items with a musical theme took up more space than the instruments offered for sale.

"You've made some changes since your father's day."

"A few."

Genuinely curious now, she explored further, enchanted by a display of ceramic and pewter figurines. Russ's stock came in all sizes and shapes and ranged from a comic dancing dog playing a drum to a eight-inch-high bisque figure of a Scotsman seated on a stump to play the bagpipes.

"A piper," she murmured. "Why am I not surprised?"

"I wish someone would buy that."

Russ's voice came from right behind her, making her jump. She hadn't realized he was so close to her in the narrow aisle she'd wandered into.

"It's completely inaccurate," he continued. "The Uilleann pipes are played sitting down, but not the Great Highland Bagpipe."

Although Tory didn't have a clue what he was talking about, she decided hearing him talk about music was preferable to another awkward silence. And much safer than discussing children, beauty pageants, or Russ's late wife.

"I suppose you sell bagpipes," she said, "and give lessons."

"In the market?" he asked, taking her by the elbow to steer her toward the rear of the shop. At the end of the aisle, two sets of pipes hung against the paneling on the back wall, one on either side of a tall, narrow window. On the shelves below were stacked boxes labeled PRACTICE CHANTER and all around and between were trophies, plaques, and ribbons, awards won at piping competitions.

When Russ was distracted by the sounds of his daughter's return, Tory took a closer look. Only this past summer, Russ had taken a first place at the Highland Games at Maine's Thomas Point Beach. Amanda had come in third in both reels and strathspeys in her division at Quechee, Vermont.

"What do you think, Daddy?" Amanda asked.

From the amount of time it took Russ to find something to say, Tory suspected he wasn't entirely pleased by their selection, though the pale green gown, with its scoop neckline and puffed sleeves, was both modest and completely appropriate for someone Amanda's age. It was floor-length, however, and Amanda's matching high heels added a good three inches to her height. She was having a little difficulty walking in them, but she'd insisted she had to have those particular shoes. Tory hadn't had the heart to say no.

Just as Russ was about to voice an opinion, Tory jabbed him in the ribs and spoke to him in a whisper. "Trust me," she said. "This is as demure as it gets. Amanda's first choice was a hot little backless number with a slit skirt. In flame-colored velour."

Russ swallowed hard. Tory was close enough to see the muscles beneath his long cotton sleeves bunch and then relax as he made an effort to revise his first answer and instead tell his daughter what she wanted to hear.

"It's very nice, honey," he finally managed.

He even sounded as if he might mean it. "Spin around so I can get the whole effect."

And check for a back, Tory thought, stifling a snicker.

The glance Russ shot her way was an odd mixture of gratitude and annoyance. "I guess it isn't so bad," he admitted in a voice too low for Amanda to hear. "But don't go tarting her up with a lot of makeup. In fact, I don't see why she needs any makeup at all. I'd rather she did without."

Tory waited until Amanda had gone back into the office to change from the dress into her jeans and sweatshirt, then she lit into Russ. "Stop issuing edicts when you don't have the slightest idea what you're talking about," she hissed.

"What?"

"No makeup," she muttered. "Sheesh!"

A customer came into the store, but Russ didn't move. Looming over her, he demanded, "Why does she need makeup?"

"Because onstage, under the lights, someone without any makeup looks as if she has no facial features whatsoever. I swear I won't overdo it, but Amanda needs blush, some eyeliner and mascara, and a pale shade of lipstick."

Without committing himself, Russ stalked away to tend to his customer. Two more came in a minute later, a young couple, and then a third, a man on his own. Leaf-peepers looking for souvenirs at the end their day, Tory guessed, and glanced at her watch. It was nearly closing time, but Russ was too good a businessman to hurry them along.

Left to her own devices, she drifted toward the window at the rear of the shop. She glanced out, then beat a hasty retreat, fighting an unexpected attack of vertigo. She'd looked directly down into the rushing waters of Waycross Stream.

Back at the front of the store, she saw that more customers had come in. Tory was struck anew by how time-consuming running the business must be. It amazed her that Russ still managed to have such a good relationship with Amanda. She doubted he was left with very many free hours, not once he'd met all his obligations as a parent.

Remember that, she cautioned herself.

She'd known all along that Tandy's Music and Gifts was a one-man operation. She assumed Russ occasionally employed help, but she also remembered that when he'd wanted to talk to her the previous Saturday he'd had to recruit Beva to mind the store.

She considered ducking out while he was busy. She'd fulfilled her obligations to Amanda for the day. Instead she pitched in, bagging purchases while Amanda ran the cash register and Russ answered questions, located merchandise, and made sales. What choice did she have? A good neighbor lent a hand. The natives of Waycross Springs came to one another's aid without waiting to be asked.

Twenty minutes later Russ flipped the "Closed" side of the sign to face outward. It was already dark beyond the glass.

"Thanks, Tory."

"You're welcome, but Amanda did most of the work." Tory came up beside him as he finished locking up.

"At least you look like a salesclerk." In response to her questioning glance, he checked to make sure Amanda was busy collecting her shopping bags and wouldn't overhear, then whispered, "This store has always had a dress code for its salespeople. No jeans allowed."

For a second she thought he was kidding, especially since Amanda's jeans were clean, unripped, and actually fit the way they were supposed to, but his serious expression quickly convinced her otherwise. "Why, for heaven's sake? Every other store in town is decidedly casual."

Even at the bridal shop where they'd found Amanda's gown, the salesclerk had been sporting denim. Tory, wearing another of her silk blouses—chosen because they could be packed without undue wrinkling—and one of her pant suits, a lightweight blue-and-white check, had spent most of the afternoon feeling overdressed. At one point she'd even caught herself thinking how glad she was that she hadn't accessorized with gold jewelry, the way she would have if she'd worn the same outfit to work.

"Call it tradition," Russ said in answer to her question. "Do you remember my grandfather? Granddad never even took his suit coat off when he was at work."

"I remember he always wore one of those bolo ties from the Southwest too. Even as a kid, I thought that was a little odd for a New Englander."

"Everyone's entitled to a small eccentricity. My father relaxed enough to wear a blazer. And sometimes he'd use one of those clip-on bow ties. I go so far as to take my jacket off when I'm at work, but that's as informal as I'm prepared to be."

Tory patted him lightly on the cheek. "That's right, Russ. You stick to your guns. Time enough to go completely casual when Amanda takes over the family business."

Before she could pull back her hand, he captured it. Tory froze as currents of awareness suddenly pulsed between them. She tugged, but he did not release her. Warily, she tilted her head the few inches necessary to meet his eyes and watched in fascination as his pupils slowly dilated.

"Funny," she murmured, "you don't look the sort to be all stuffy and conservative." The breathless quality was back in her voice. She closed her eyes in a futile attempt to hide her reaction. She was more successful at holding back a moan.

"Only about clothes," he said close to her ear. "Get me out of them and—"

"I'm hungry," Amanda announced in an impatient voice.

The scenes playing on the backs of Tory's eyelids splintered. She sucked in a sharp breath. The urge to moan had been replaced by a desire to howl in frustration.

"I'm hungry too," Russ said loudly enough for Amanda to hear. Then his voice went low and raspy again. Intimate. "Very hungry."

There was no mistaking his double meaning. Tory's eyes flew open.

"You've got to come with us, Tory," Amanda said, closer now. In another minute she'd be standing right next to them. "We've still got stuff to talk about."

Tory started to stutter an excuse, but Russ squeezed the hand he continued to hold. "Have supper with us," he invited. "Consider it partial repayment for all you've done for Amanda today."

Had she imagined his need? When Tory blinked and looked again, she could find no trace of passion in Russ's bland expression.

He released her hand, but her fingers still tingled.

"Can we go to Aphrodite's?" Amanda asked. "Please, Daddy."

"Where else?"

"Tory?" Amanda prompted her.

"Resistance is useless," Russ put in. "Amanda won't stop nagging until you give in and agree."

Striving to match his casual tone and go him one better, Tory acquiesced. "Fine," she said, "as long as we don't go anywhere really fancy." She forced a teasing smile. "Wouldn't want anyone to tell me I'm not dressed for it."

A short time later the three of them were seated in a booth at Aphrodite's. It turned out to be a pizza parlor, its name explained by the fact that it was run by Waycross Springs' only family of Greek descent. Tory ordered a hamburger.

"Hamburger," she repeated when Russ quirked a brow at her. "Well done."

She was too rattled by their exchange in the store to risk anything else on the menu. Nervous as she was—her hands were still trembling and she couldn't quite convince herself it was from the cold outside—she'd probably end up wearing her supper if she ordered spaghetti, and in the past, even when she wasn't shaky, pizza toppings had shown an alarming tendency to slide off onto her blouse or into her lap.

"So, is the clothes shopping finished?" Russ asked when they'd all given their orders and Amanda had left them to talk to some girls her own age. The restaurant seemed to be popular with young people, Tory noticed, both with their families and on their own.

"I think we've thought of everything." She dug the sales slips out of her purse and handed them over. Most of the items Amanda had selected had been put on his charge card. A few, the most frivolous of the lot, Tory had paid for herself, giving in to the temptation to make gifts of them to her young friend.

"What did you buy besides the gown and shoes?" Russ tucked the receipts away without even glancing at them.

"The dreaded makeup and a casual outfit," she answered. "There is no swimsuit competition, thank goodness, and when I picked Amanda up at your house, she showed me her costume for the talent portion. That plaid skirt and sash look very nice on her."

The girl had insisted upon modeling the outfit, dithering about which hat to wear. One was called a Glengarry, the other a Balmoral, but Tory couldn't have said which was which now if her life depended upon it. All she remembered was that one sported a feather. A cockade, Amanda had called it.

Tory had been hoping to see more of the Tandy house than Amanda's room, just to satisfy her curiosity without actually spending time there in Russ's company, but she'd glimpsed little else beyond the front stairs and two hallways, one downstairs and one up.

"Kilt, not skirt. Tartan, not plaid," Russ corrected her. "And the name for the sash is spelled the same as plaid but it's pronounced 'played.' It's actually a rectangular wool cape in a tartan pattern, designed to be worn over one shoulder."

"If you say so. The point is, the outfit flatters Amanda."

"The point is, it looks *authentic* on Amanda, though I suppose that if we were going strictly by the rules, no female would wear a kilt at all, let alone play the bagpipes. It's an instrument of war, you know."

"And just who drew up those rules?" Tory asked. Russ looked so earnest that she couldn't resist teasing him, even knowing where a similar conversation had led them just a short while ago at the store.

"Warriors, of course."

"Of course. I should have guessed. I did see *Braveheart*."

He winced.

"Let me guess. Not authentic?"

"Wrong kind of bagpipes."

"Ah." Obviously the reason the hero of the piece had to die.

When Tory spotted their waitress emerging from the kitchen with what appeared to be their order, she looked around for Amanda. She was talking to a boy. No, flirting with him. And if Tory was any judge, the girl standing behind Amanda didn't care for what she was seeing.

As Tory watched, the boy left with several of his friends. Amanda headed for the rest room.

The jealous girl, accompanied by another, was right on her heels.

Tory didn't like the odds.

"I need to wash up," she said, cutting into Russ's enumeration of other historical and musical inaccuracies committed by filmmakers in movies about Scotland. "Be right back."

Mere seconds before the waitress arrived with their food, Tory ducked out of the booth. She pushed open the ladies'-room door just in time to hear a high-pitched female voice begin to chant.

"Mandy Tandy. Pudding and pie," the girl misquoted. "Kissed the boys and made them cry."

" 'Cuz she's so ugly," her crony elaborated, sneering.

"Pretty is as pretty does," Amanda shot back.

All three of them stood in front of the mirror, pretending their only reason for being there was to fuss with their hair.

You go, girl, Tory thought. Maybe Amanda didn't need a defender after all.

An abrupt silence fell when they realized an adult had invaded the precincts. Tory made a production out of sauntering up to the sink to wash her hands. She was still rinsing when the two girls who had been taunting Amanda slammed out of the rest room, leaving Tory alone with Russ's daughter.

Amanda would not meet her eyes. "I didn't need any help," she mumbled, giving one last lick to her hair with a brush. Static snapped and the strands refused to lie flat.

"I could see that." Tory waited a beat. "Nice to know some things never change." Instead of drying her hands, she stroked her damp palms over Amanda's rebellious locks, taming the flyaway ends.

"What do you mean?" Amanda asked. "What doesn't change?"

"Other kids used to call me Icky Vicki when I was your age. And Vicki Mouse."

And Brainiac, she added to herself. The old saw about sticks and stones might be true in the physical sense, but she remembered how much words could hurt, especially when one was young and insecure.

"But your name isn't Vicki." Amanda sounded confused, but if she'd been deeply affected by the girls' barbs, Tory saw no evidence of it now. A puzzled frown had replaced the earlier pained expression.

"It was back then," Tory told her. "Both Vicki and Tory are common nicknames for Victoria."

Amanda thought that over. "When I have children of my own, I'm going to be very careful what I call them. No rhymes."

Good luck, Tory thought. Kids were creative when it came to inventing taunts. In Amanda's case, though, they hadn't had far to look. What on earth had Russ and his wife been thinking?

"Were you named after your mother?" she asked.

"Nope. Her name was Melody."

"Pretty name," Tory said.

Amanda only shrugged, but as they exited the ladies' room, Tory was sure she heard the girl mutter the same words she'd uttered earlier: "Pretty is as pretty does."

"It's no bother for me to drive you home," Russ insisted some two hours later. They'd walked back to the store to pick up his car, then had driven to his house so Amanda could give Tory a photo of herself, one taken at the Quechee competition. At dinner, the two of them had decided this picture would be featured in Amanda's brochure.

Russ didn't approve of those brochures, or of the idea that his daughter would be soliciting contributions from other merchants in town. Tory had made the process sound harmless enough, but now, watching Tory shiver as she stood on his front porch, clutching the photograph and repeatedly declining his offer, he had to wonder if she had as much common sense as he'd believed.

"Russ, it's only a few blocks," she repeated for at least the tenth time. "I can walk."

"You don't have a coat," he reminded her. Her suit jacket was clearly inadequate against the evening chill.

"I didn't need one earlier. The temperature topped out at nearly sixty degrees today."

"In case you haven't noticed, the sun has been down for some time. It's darned close to freezing now and the wind is picking up."

"Fine! Drive me home!" She sounded irritable, but as she turned to hurry down the sidewalk to his car, he thought he heard her chuckle.

"What?"

"Nothing."

He didn't pursue it, or her. Instead he ducked into the house and called upstairs to tell Amanda he was taking Tory home and would be back in a few minutes.

That was likely to be the literal truth. It was only a short distance from his place, at the corner of Kincaid Street and North Road, to her house on Elm. Nothing in Waycross Springs was very far from anything else.

But when he pulled in at curbside, Russ knew he didn't want to leave her just yet. And when he judged that she meant to bolt—she released her seat belt before he'd even come to a full stop—he decided he wanted to know just what she'd found so amusing back there on his front porch.

He caught her left hand as her right hand touched the handle of the passenger-side door. "Why the chuckle?" he asked. "What's so funny about me driving you home?"

At first he didn't think she was going to answer. Then she turned so that she could look at him. Her face was difficult to see, since the only light came from the faint beams of a street lamp two doors down, but he could swear she was blushing.

"You must have known I had a crush on you in high school."

"Did you?" He felt ridiculously pleased. He shouldn't be. After the ludicrous thoughts he'd had about her the day before she left for Ireland, he'd tried hard to stifle any tendency to think and react like a teenager when he was around her.

"Oh, yes," she assured him. "Big time. And to that foolish teenage girl, dinner tonight at what's obviously a teenage hangout and now—be still my beating heart!—you driving me home, well, that would have made all my adolescent dreams come true."

Although she was plainly trying to sound as if this were all a big joke to her, Russ sensed there was more than a little genuine emotion tangled up in her words. "I wish I'd known how you felt back then," he said.

"That would have been the final humiliation."

"I'd never have done anything to hurt you," he protested.

"Yeah, right! Get real, Russ. You might not have meant to be cruel, but you'd have laughed your head off at the thought of mousy little Vicki MacDougall lusting after the big basketball star."

Unable to deny the truth of her charge, he said

only, "Teenage boys aren't noted for their sensitivity."

"And you were probably a bit egotistical about your success with girls. From what I remember hearing, your dates usually got a lot more than dinner and a ride home."

As soon as the words were out, she looked stricken. "Can I take back that last part?"

Too late, Russ thought. In spite of his best efforts, he was feeling a lot like the high-school kid she was describing. He'd been a bit of a hellraiser, he acknowledged, in a quiet, small-town way. And he'd never been able to resist a challenge, especially one issued by an attractive girl.

"So, Vicki," he teased. "Exactly how would this dream date of ours have ended?"

He didn't give her time to speak, certain he knew what her answer would be . . . if she were honest. Using the grip he still had on her hand, he tugged her toward him, leaning in at the same time to bring their lips together.

He'd meant to make the kiss light, a gesture of friendship, an acknowledgment of shared memories of a time when they hadn't been more than passing acquaintances.

Or so he thought until his mouth actually touched hers.

In that instant everything but the contact between them faded away. Her lips were as soft as they'd looked, and welcoming. Her scent surrounded him. Suddenly there was no past, no future, no present beyond the front seat of his car.

He'd kissed women before. A fair number of them. He couldn't remember ever being so overwhelmed by that one simple act. In a strange way, it was like the first kiss two innocents shared. Magical. Memorable.

It rapidly became more intricate, shattering all his preconceived notions about what a kiss could be, and about what he felt for Tory Grenville.

She felt it, too, he was certain. They clung to each other, his arms at her waist, hers circling his neck. The kiss intensified, tiny mutual nibbles at lips deepening into the first tentative explorations of mouths with tongues.

At seventeen, he'd have been trying to get her beneath him about now. Making out, they'd called it back then. Heavy petting. But that wasn't enough for the man he had become. And with this woman, the "more" he wanted was infinitely complex, in part physical, but in large measure emotional too.

Frenzied, they touched and caressed, never once letting their lips separate. Mutual passion drove them on until Russ's hand slid up under the blouse and camisole he'd tugged out of her waistband, and for the first time he touched the underside of her bare breast.

Abruptly, she stiffened in his arms, then pulled away.

He freed her instantly, though his body throbbed with unfulfilled desire.

She wouldn't look at him again. This time her fumbling with the door handle got it open on the first try and she was out of the car in an instant. A moment later she'd fled up the sidewalk to her front porch.

"Damn," Russ muttered. He'd tried to devour her. No wonder she'd pushed him away and bolted.

Confused, aroused, wondering if he'd just wrecked any possibility of friendship between them, he watched Tory until she was safely inside the house. As soon as the lights came on in her living room, he forced himself to put the car into drive and pull away from the curb.

He didn't want to leave. But if he went after her now, it would not be to apologize.

It would be to finish what they'd started.

FIVE

In her tiny home office, Tory put the finishing touches on Amanda's brochure, using the equipment her company had provided so that its sales force could produce classy-looking visual aids and reports. It had taken longer than she'd expected to design the thrice-folded, two-sided flyer. She'd used this particular computer program only once or twice. More commonly, she used the computer to do word processing, spreadsheets, and E-mail.

Satisfied with the results of her morning's work, she ran off twenty copies of the brochure, designed to convince local businessmen to back Amanda's bid to become a beauty queen. When the printer stopped spitting out pages, she squared the corners and slid the entire stack into an empty paper box. The task of folding she'd leave to Russ's daughter.

You're just looking for an excuse to go over there, she chastised herself.

Even before last night, she'd been having trouble getting Russ out of her thoughts. That kiss had boggled her mind. All night long, both when she was awake and in her dreams, she'd replayed those few minutes of ecstasy. Morning had found her lying amid tangled sheets, hot and bothered and calling herself six kinds of fool.

He'd caught her off guard. She'd been so sure he wasn't interested in her, even after that strange interlude at closing time in the store. And then . . . the kiss that should not have happened. The kiss she should never have allowed.

She didn't like kissing. Never had.

Yeah, right.

She'd liked it just fine with Russ.

Maybe that was what upset her most. She'd actually been able to imagine liking the rest of what two passionate people did together.

Deliberately, she turned her thoughts to her marriage to Chad Grenville. Ordinarily that was enough to make her want to swear off men, but this time the memories backfired. She still recalled everything clearly, but now she was able to see his behavior, hear his taunting words, from a new perspective. For reasons of his own, reasons she'd never fully understood, Chad had wooed her, won her, wed her, all without more than the most perfunctory of sexual preliminaries.

He'd said he wanted her to save herself for her

wedding day, that he respected the fact she was still a virgin, but their marriage had never been about respect. It had been about control.

The revelation stunned Tory. She'd married a cold fish, believing they'd discover passion together. When what happened in the bedroom had disappointed them both, she'd accepted his verdict that it was her fault, that she did not like sex, that she was frigid.

How dumb could a woman be?

The problem had not been with her, but with him. And with Russ there didn't appear to be any problem at all.

Except that entering a new relationship on the rebound was a really lousy idea.

"Mustn't forget that," she muttered to herself as she left her office.

Damn shame, she thought as she fed the cats, then collected her coat, the box of flyers, and a notepad.

It didn't matter that kissing Russ made her toes curl and kicked her metabolism into overdrive. She was not in the market for a romance right now. They were working together for Amanda's sake. Nothing more.

She'd do well to remember that.

Before she lost her nerve, she had to go over there and face the man who'd unknowingly changed the way she felt about sex. She had to keep her hormones under control and her lips to herself and prove to both of them that she could take his impulsive kiss in stride, that she was unembarrassed, unaffected, unruffled, undaunted by the prospect of working closely with him for another five weeks.

"You are sophisticated. Together. With it," she chanted as she set out along Elm Street.

Sunday, his only day off, was the time Russ set aside to spend with Amanda. It was the day he tried to be both father and mother, he thought, smiling wryly as he checked the stew simmering in the slow cooker. He had fresh rolls from Glendorra's to go with it. Later he'd toss a salad.

There was enough for three, he realized when he responded to a hesitant tapping at the kitchen entrance and recognized Tory Grenville through the semisheer curtain drawn across the glass. It took him aback that inviting her to dinner was his first thought.

His second was that she looked just as appealing with sunlight bringing out the russet highlights in her hair as she had lit only by a street lamp.

He opened the door.

She held up a white box, the kind expensive business stationery came in. "Brochures," she announced. "Is Amanda home?"

He nodded and stepped aside to let her into the kitchen, noticing as he did just how well she fit into their surroundings. She even matched the color scheme. The dark green of her outfit was almost identical to the shade his mother had chosen years earlier to trim the cabinets. The pattern on the window curtains picked up the amber of her hazel eyes and the chestnut hues in her hair.

Russ shook his head to clear it. He was getting fanciful.

Getting? His imagination had been running wild ever since he'd gone to this woman's house a little over a week ago. Behave, he warned himself. She was just someone who'd agreed to help his daughter. She was there with the brochures she'd put together for Amanda, not to see Amanda's father.

If her reaction last night was any guide, she'd have been happy never to cross paths with him again.

She didn't seem to be embarrassed, though. His eyes narrowed speculatively. She ought to be feeling something, revealing something of how she felt. That she could hide her emotions so well was not a good sign.

Melody had also been an expert at concealing her reactions.

"Sit," he invited, indicating the kitchen table. "Coffee?"

"Amanda," she reminded him, but she seated herself and plunked the box down in front of her. Her purse landed with a thump on the floor beside her chair.

"Upstairs. On the phone." He felt his features

alter into a woebegone expression. "In that respect alone, I guess I have to allow that she's almost a teenager. She's already lobbying for her own private line."

"Good for her." Tory's answering smile looked a little stiff. He told himself that finding this small chink in her armor was better than nothing.

"I figure you're ticked off at me," he said as he poured two cups of coffee from the big pot he kept going all day on Sundays. He handed one to her and sat down opposite her with the other. "You've got good cause to be. I shouldn't have grabbed you that way. I'm—"

"Oh, for heaven's sake! Don't apologize. You were only fulfilling my girlhood fantasy." She picked up the mug and took a sip, pretending to be completely absorbed in the activity.

Too late, Russ realized he'd given her the mug labeled HERS. He glanced down and winced when he saw the word HIS inscribed on the one in his hand.

"Ever think maybe my fantasies were involved there too?" he asked in a quiet voice.

Her smile brightened by a few notches. He had the uneasy feeling it was all for show. She was not comfortable about what had happened between them. Neither was he. Perversely, it pleased him to discover he was not alone in that.

He started to speak, but she held up a hand. A gloved hand, he noticed, though the day was another nice one. At least fifty degrees outside. She hadn't taken off her coat either.

"We were satisfying a bit of curiosity left over from high school," she said firmly. "I admit it rattled me for a moment, but we're hardly kids now." She forced a chuckle, as if it had all been a big joke.

"Are you sure about that?"

"Have I completely misread you?" she asked. "I mean, you certainly seemed interested last night, but I was under the impression that you . . . well . . ."

"What?" He was genuinely curious, and pleased to see that she'd stopped trying to hide behind a social mask. With a soft sigh, she shrugged out of her light coat and removed the gloves.

"Cards on the table?" she asked.

"Please."

"You reacted rather strongly the other day, when Ms. Arsenica thought we were married. I assumed that meant I didn't compare well to Melody."

For some reason he could not fathom, Russ suddenly wanted to be open with Tory, to explain himself and clear the air between them. Cards on the table, as she'd said.

If nothing else, it was damned awkward not being certain how much she knew, or had guessed, about his late wife. Small-town gossip being what it was, she'd have only had to ask in order to hear all kinds of stories. A few of them might be accurate. Most, he suspected, would not be.

"My wife was in the process of leaving me when she died," he said bluntly. Tory's eyes widened. "She wanted to 'find herself.'" He heard the bitterness in his own voice, saw his hands clench into fists on the table before he spat out the rest. "If she hadn't died in a traffic accident, we'd have been divorced now."

"And Amanda?"

"Amanda would still be living with me. Melody didn't want her. Worse, she told Amanda so before she left."

For a moment renewed anger at his former spouse held him gripped in its claws. Then he forced himself to go on. He wanted Tory to know everything.

"Melody made a point of trying to justify her actions to Amanda before she took off." That was only one of the things for which Russ had trouble forgiving his late wife. "It's a miracle my daughter turned out to be as well adjusted as she is. Melody's desertion might have left much worse scars."

"Pretty is as pretty does," Tory murmured.

"My mother's expression."

Russ didn't have to ask Tory where she'd heard it, but he frowned when he considered a new implication of the old saw Amanda had picked up from her paternal grandmother. Was Melody's desertion the real reason Amanda felt compelled to prove herself by entering a beauty pageant? He hoped not.

"I'm so sorry." Tory's hand covered one of his fists. That simple gesture of sympathy and understanding surprised him and seemed to startle her as well.

Fascinated by the textures of her skin, the feeling of her fingers wrapped around his, he shifted their clasped hands until he was the one holding her. Little electric shocks sparked between them as he ran his thumb lazily down her palm to the frantically beating pulse at her wrist.

When he realized what he was doing, what he was feeling, he released her. Simultaneously, they both removed their hands from the tabletop. His hung, clenched, at his sides. He suspected hers were tightly entwined on her lap.

"Have you always lived in this house?" she asked in a blatant attempt to bring the conversation back to neutral territory. In a way he was surprised she didn't just abandon him and go looking for Amanda. After all, it was his daughter she'd come to see.

Wasn't it?

"We moved in when Amanda was two." He kept his voice as casual as he could, a neat trick when simply being in the same room with Tory continued to have a noticeable effect on certain portions of his anatomy. "Melody hated the place where we lived when we were first married. I'm not sure she liked this house much better, but she didn't change anything." He gestured broadly, taking in the whole kitchen, the whole house. "What you see is the way my mother decorated it."

"You must have married young."

He took a long swallow of coffee. "Anyone in town can tell you the statistics. I was twenty. Still going to college over to Fallstown. Too young and stupid to know better than to fall for a pretty face."

"Age doesn't necessarily lead to good decisions," Tory told him.

"Why? How old were you when you married?"

"Old enough to know better," she shot back. She sipped, then put the mug down with a thump and looked him straight in the eye. "I waited for Mr. Right and I thought I'd found him, but he was all show and no substance. The marriage lasted three years. During most of that time I made myself completely miserable trying to please him."

"I hear you," he said. And he understood . . . with a vengeance.

"I guess you do." She seemed to relax again.

"Amanda has been my priority since her mother left. Amanda first, the business second. Between those two things, I haven't had time or inclination to pursue relationships with women. Still don't. I didn't take kindly to the notion that

Beva was trying to set us up, although when I called her on it, she made sure I knew you'd been through a rough divorce and weren't looking."

"I'm on the rebound," Tory said frankly, "which means my emotions are completely untrustworthy. So even if you think I'm interested in you, even if I think I am, the attraction we feel is unlikely to be more than a passing fancy. Certainly not enough to risk getting . . . involved. I'd say we've both been hurt enough. Why ask for more pain?"

"Well, that seems to say it all." Her body language, however, contradicted her words.

He had to hide a satisfied smile when he noticed that she'd slid her right shoe partway off her foot, balancing it precariously on the tips of her toes. According to a book he'd once read, that meant she was comfortable in his presence . . . and possibly coming on to him, though she was probably unaware of that herself.

"Yes." She slid the shoe back on. "So. We'd do well to restrict our relationship to—"

"Friendship?"

Without showing any teeth, she smiled. "Is it true that there's nothing worse for a teenage boy than being told by the object of his affection that she likes him only as a friend?"

"True for a teenager of either sex, I imagine. But, Tory, we aren't teenagers anymore."

"And neither one of us really wants anything more than friendship," she insisted.

That's what you think. But he nodded.

"You have to put Amanda first and the store second," she said, quoting his own words back at him. "And from what Amanda has told me, from what I've observed for myself, no girl could have a better father."

He acknowledged her praise with another nod, though he knew he had many shortcomings. He stood and went to the counter to refill his mug. Tory hadn't touched her coffee after the first few sips.

"Do you suppose Amanda's off the phone by now?" she asked.

He hoped not. Russ didn't want his daughter to join them just yet, even if his tête-à-tête with Tory was to be only a platonic interlude in his mother's kitchen. "Why don't you show me what you've got for her before she comes downstairs?"

"I folded one of the brochures and left the rest for Amanda to do." Tory opened the box and extracted the flyer as he came up beside her, coffee in hand.

He winced. The front featured that photograph of Amanda in the tuxedo, the one where she looked far too old and far too sophisticated. "What kind of photographer takes a twelve-year-old girl and turns her into a sex kitten?"

Tory laughed out loud. "In this case, one who believes the customer is always right. That's the outfit and hairstyle Amanda chose. Alexa just took the picture."

"Posed it."

"Well, yes. She's quite the one for shoving and prodding her subjects into position. But Amanda came up with that sultry look all on her own. Probably saw it on some movie or television star's face."

"Movie star, huh? Not Alexa herself?"

"Good heavens, no! Alexa looks like the Pillsbury Doughboy in a caftan."

"I stand corrected."

"Good. Now put your coffee down and look at the rest of the brochure. I think it came out quite well."

Inside, things did improve. Tory had used the candid shot Amanda had fetched for her the night before, the photograph taken just after she won third prize for her piping at Quechee. His daughter was literally grinning from ear to ear. All kid.

The text of the pamphlet was also tasteful, even if it had been designed to solicit money. As required by the pageant, the letter accepting Amanda as a contestant and explaining the fund-raising rules was printed in full. The back flap contained two paragraphs Amanda had composed to introduce herself to prospective backers.

"I didn't edit this." Tory tapped the brief bio. "I thought it should sound like a twelve-year-old wrote it."

He'd been leaning over her shoulder to study the brochure. Gradually, Russ's awareness of the printed words faded and Tory seeped into his senses.

She didn't smell earthy today, he realized. And she wasn't wearing the light, flowery scent she'd had on the night before, either. But he inhaled something appealing. Something with . . . cinnamon?

She'd had a sticky bun for breakfast. He'd bet on it. Would she still taste like cinnamon and sugar? He badly wanted to find out. Toothpaste flavor would be okay too. Or mouthwash. In fact—

Without warning, as if she'd read his thoughts, she put some distance between them by dragging her purse from the floor up onto the table and burrowing into it.

"We need to discuss the schedule leading up to the pageant," she said. "I have to leave town in a week. I'll be gone several days. Other than that, I'm at your disposal."

"I like the sound of that."

The quick burst of color in her cheeks delighted him. "In your dreams," she muttered.

All too likely, he thought as he forced himself to behave. Seducing a woman in his kitchen with his daughter just upstairs was out. Seducing this one anywhere after the little heart-to-heart they'd just had was not a very good idea.

But he hadn't felt this alive since Melody left. He decided he liked it.

Too bad the object of his interest was so determined not to be enticed into anything more than friendship.

"Schedule it is," he agreed, and retrieved the list he'd compiled earlier in the day. At the same moment that he held his paper out for Tory's inspection, she whipped a pad of paper from that oversize purse and shoved it toward him. They both froze for a moment. Then the corner of her mouth twitched.

Laughter rang out in the old kitchen, shattering the tension that had started to develop between them. By the time they recovered, it was easy to keep smiling.

"Okay," she said. "Let's see what your number-one priority is."

He'd written on the back of an old circular. She turned it around, read the words, then chuckled. "Return shoes?"

"I can live with the dress, but those heels make her look too grown up."

"You'll have to work that one out with Amanda."

"Coward."

She ignored the taunt and studied the remaining items on his list, saying nothing. He'd concentrated on the things that bothered him about the pageant—the clothes, the makeup, the attempt to turn girls into living dolls.

At the same time he perused Tory's list, which was actually a schedule. She'd listed items by date:

November 2: money due
November 14: afternoon: training session
(Carstairs Hotel, Portland) evening:
participants-only party
November 21: rehearsal (Sinclair House)
November 22: pageant

"Those are the highlights," she said. "That
session in Portland is only four weeks away. It's a
Saturday, so I imagine you'll need to work, but I
can take Amanda. They won't let any parents attend the party, anyway. Apparently that's when
the girls decide which of their fellow contestants
win the congeniality awards in each division."

He could take some time off, Russ thought,
but he didn't commit himself. He didn't like to
make promises he wasn't sure he'd be able to
keep. But he wanted to be there for his little girl,
even if he didn't entirely approve of what she was
doing.

"I'd feel better if you and Amanda stayed over-
night in Portland," he heard himself say. "Instead
of driving back late at night."

"That's sensible," Tory agreed. "And a hotel
room might be nice. Someplace to go while
Amanda's at that party." She grinned at him. "I'm
not the type to hang out in a lobby bar while I'm
waiting."

"No way am I touching that line."

Her grin widened. "Coward."

Russ decided he was beginning to like this

comfortable new rapport between them. Friendship? He supposed it was. For the moment he set aside any other thoughts generated by being this close to her and tapped her list with the eraser end of his pencil.

"When is your Houston trip?"

"I leave a week from today."

"Need a ride to the airport?"

"I don't want to impose."

"Call it a trade."

She looked wary again. "For what?"

"You can help me out when you come back, if you're free on the fifth. Save me from those matchmakers we're both so wary of. Like Beva, for example." She started to protest, but he cut her off. "It won't really be a date, but if you're with me, that will save me explaining why I didn't bring one. It's just the annual local small-business-association dinner. No big deal." He sent her his most winning smile.

She hesitated a moment longer, then relented. "Okay, but—"

The ringing phone cut her off, and he was glad of it, but his elation faded as soon as the caller identified herself. He was frowning by the time he hung up.

"Who was that?" Tory asked.

"Reporter from the *Waycross Springs Gazette*. She wants to do a piece on Amanda."

"That's great."

"You think so?"

"I think Amanda will."

"This particular reporter is also a stringer for the paper in Three Cities."

Tory nodded, indicating her familiarity with the regional section of that newspaper. The local paper was a weekly, and the county was also served by a biweekly published in Fallstown. "It only makes sense that they want to play up the local-contestant angle. Let's get Amanda down here, since she's obviously finished her phone call, and ask her what she thinks." Tory gestured toward the box. "She needs to get started folding flyers too."

"Stay and have dinner with us," he invited. "It's probably ready." They did eat early on Sundays. He hoped the stew had finished cooking.

Before she could decline the invitation, he went in search of Amanda. He found his daughter just about to descend the stairs, and for an uneasy moment wondered if she'd been lurking, eavesdropping on their conversation.

Things went downhill from there.

Amanda had an oddly subdued reaction to the news that she was about to become famous, and that cast a decided pall over dinner. The meal itself wasn't his best. The meat was done, but he'd cut the potatoes into overlarge sections, thinking they'd cook several hours longer. To say they were crunchy was putting a flattering face on the situation.

The conversation didn't suit his taste either.

From their discussion of how it would be best for Amanda to approach the businesses on the square, he got the impression his daughter meant to solicit every shop along East Depot, Park, Grove, and Middle streets. Tory suggested she also visit the Sinclair House.

Russ tried to get into the spirit of the thing. He mentioned Glendorra's and Aphrodite's. Then he made the mistake of advising Amanda to stop in at the newspaper office.

His daughter had already finished eating. She shoved her chair away from the table, mumbled something about having to phone Jolene, and fled.

"I wonder what that's all about?" Tory mused. "Why should the prospect of being interviewed in the local paper bother a self-confident, outgoing child like Amanda?"

"Darned if I know." Together they cleared the table and started the dishes. "And why call Jolene? I guess you've heard that Beva's daughter doesn't approve of beauty pageants."

"I know. Her mother told me she thinks she's raised a feminist. She doesn't seem sure whether to be pleased or alarmed."

Their hands met in the soapy water in the sink. Gazes locked. Something in her eyes told Russ she was remembering the kiss they'd shared in the front seat of his car. He remembered it, too, every passionate moment of it, and his body hardened in a rush.

Tory jerked away from him as if she'd been

burned. Refusing to look at him again, she quickly withdrew. "I'm just in the way here," she said, seizing a hand towel to dry off.

"Not at all."

"I need to get home anyway." She sent him a too bright smile. "Got to feed the cats."

Before he could think of anything to say that would stop her, she had shrugged into her coat and gloves and was out the door. "Tell Amanda I'll see her tomorrow," she called back over her shoulder.

Russ looked down at the dishpan. Soapsuds covered his arms halfway to the elbows. He'd tied a dish towel around his waist to keep from splashing water on the front of his jeans. He'd make a fine sight, chasing Tory Grenville down the street.

"I ought to be used to women running out on me by now," he grumbled under his breath. Then, hearing his own words, he had to laugh. Poor Russ. Feeling sorry for himself.

What a waste of time.

Almost as much a waste as settling for nothing more than friendship with Tory Grenville.

Monday, Tory had her work to keep her busy all day. She maintained her focus until she stopped for a coffee break halfway through the afternoon.

Big mistake.

From the moment she glanced at her watch

and realized that Amanda had just gotten out of school and was about to start going door-to-door with her brochures, she could not concentrate on anything but the girl . . . and her father.

What had happened after Sunday dinner? She could not quite put her finger on it. Before dinner, they'd talked things out. She'd thought they had agreed that simple friendship was what they both wanted.

Hah!

It was no *friend* who'd had her tossing and turning a second night in a row.

Face it, chum. You want him.

There was no sense in lying to herself. Tory had as much of a crush on the man now as when she'd been in high school.

How pathetic!

She struggled to work until her self-appointed quitting time, but when she finally shut down her computer, she went directly to her bedroom to stand in front of the closet.

She told herself she had a responsibility to check on Amanda's progress with the fund-raising, and she couldn't go out looking like this. The loose, comfortable sweats she wore when she worked at home weren't for anyone's eyes but her own.

A half hour later, wearing the same stylish wool pants and silk blouse she'd had on when she first went to Russ's house to meet Amanda, Tory hopped into her car and drove downtown. It was five-thirty, almost sunset in these last days before daylight saving ended.

This close to closing on a Monday, there were no customers in Tandy's Music and Gifts. Amanda was there, though. As Tory had expected, she had gone to the store rather than all the way to Jolene's house when she'd finished making her rounds.

What Tory had not anticipated was that Amanda would be playing a practice chanter, the instrument one used to perfect fingering for the bagpipes. Russ and Amanda, seated on two stools behind the counter, appeared to be in the middle of a music lesson. Russ glanced up at the sound of the bell above the door, but he did not stop the lesson.

"G," he instructed. "Then B. Now A. Good."

Amanda played the notes as he called them out.

"Get that pinkie all the way up," her father ordered.

Amanda complied and the lesson continued.

"Hope you weren't bored," Russ said to Tory a short time later. Still practicing, Amanda now played a tune instead of doing exercises.

"Actually, I found it fascinating," Tory said. "Must be the student."

"Or the teacher?"

"You're so modest," she teased him, relieved to find that the sense of ease between them had been restored.

Maybe her abrupt flight from his kitchen the previous afternoon hadn't been as obvious as she'd thought.

"I'm certain of one thing," she added. "It couldn't be the music."

The sound produced on the chanter was blessedly softer than that made by a real bagpipe, but both were an acquired taste.

"Tory. Tory. Tory. We've got to work on your education."

He came out from behind the counter and caught her hand, pulling her after him toward the back wall where the pipes were displayed.

"These are the drones," he said, taking one bagpipe down and touching each of its three long wooden pipes as he rested them on his left shoulder. Each had two sections and he made short work of adjusting them to tune the instrument, a maneuver that required him to blow air into a mouthpiece to fill the bag he wedged under his left arm.

The sound was . . . indescribable.

Her hands over her ears, Tory watched Russ remove the reed from the chanter, a somewhat bigger version of the one used to practice fingering. It hung from the lower end of the bag. He moistened the reed by sticking it in his mouth. She should have been disgusted, but somehow Russ made the action look erotic. Her own mouth went dry.

"A bagpipe can only produce nine notes." He

proceeded to demonstrate them at full volume
then launched into a song that sounded vaguely
familiar.

" 'Scotland the Brave,' " Amanda shouted
above the din. "Everyone plays 'Scotland the
Brave.' "

In the small store the noise was deafening.

Russ walked away from them, heading for the
front of the shop.

"It's hard to play sitting down," the girl explained. "Ya just gotta march."

"Does he have to do *that*?" Tory asked.

Russ had marched right out the door and
across East Depot Street to enter the park.

"Yeah, he does. Stuff like that used to embarrass my mother to pieces."

Startled by the comment, Tory stared at her,
but Amanda's attention had returned to her father.

"Does it embarrass you?" Tory asked.

"Nah. Besides, most of the time I'm playing
too."

"Do the kids at school give you any grief
about it?"

She shook her head, then turned to face Tory,
grinning broadly. "Of course that may only be
because when I'm in full piping regalia, I wear a
sharp little knife called a skean dhu tucked into
the top of my hose. Daddy says the legend goes
that when the English banned all weapons among
the Scots, they left them their skean dhus. Said

they were just the right size for a Scotsman to use to slit his own throat."

"Charming."

Tory's gaze shot back to Russ. He was now circling the park. She noticed he'd drawn a small, apparently appreciative crowd. At least no one was throwing drop apples at him.

He was not in Scottish dress. He hadn't even bothered with a coat, but wore his regular business outfit of dress shirt, tie, and dark slacks. But it was far too easy, with the skirling of the pipes filling the air, for Tory to visualize him in a kilt.

She'd thought about him once before in the costume Mel Gibson made famous in *Braveheart*. Now her fevered imagination supplied an open-necked pirate shirt from an old Errol Flynn movie and suddenly the whole package, even with the deafening sound effects, became infinitely appealing.

Tory sighed.

No doubt about it. This was going to be another restless night.

SIX

Fall back. Russ had always hated that phrase. But here it was, the last Sunday in October. Before going to bed, he'd set his clocks back an hour. Well before dawn, he'd gotten up to drive Tory to the airport and watch her fly out of his life for most of the next week.

During the past seven days, there had been no more close calls, not physically anyway. He'd decided he was sorry about that. He was considering a remedy, even though Tory had said she was reluctant to get romantically involved.

Russ doubted that the barriers she'd erected were very strong. He'd observed too many subtle signs to the contrary. Body language again, he thought, and grinned. He'd found that book, the one he'd first discovered when he was in the eighth grade, and taken it out of the public library to reread.

Unfortunately, the signals Tory was sending out this morning were not encouraging. She huddled on her side of the car, arms folded, legs crossed at the knees, face averted.

It had still been dark during the first part of the two-hour-plus drive from Waycross Springs. Daylight improved things very little. Not only were most of the leaves gone, which took away a good deal of the charm of any breezy, sunny autumn day, but it was also raining.

Rusty hills and dun-colored grass gave way to flat, even more uninteresting land as they left the mountains and drew near Portland. Conversation between them, which had flowed so easily for days, came in fits and starts. Tory had said little since she slipped into his car and discovered Amanda wasn't going along for the ride.

"I appreciate your giving up your day off to drive me," she said for what seemed like the thousandth time.

"I wanted to do it, okay?" After so many repetitions, he knew he sounded out of sorts.

Russ tried to fix his attention on the turnpike. Signs for south Portland, ferry terminal, and airport were followed by a depressing view of wall-to-wall shopping malls and the Sheraton Tara Hotel on one side of the road and office buildings on the other.

He went on. "There was no reason for you to take your car and pay outrageous parking fees when I have today free and Beva's going to be

down this way on the afternoon you come back."
Jolene had an appointment with some high-priced
orthodontist who likely was no better than the
man they had close by in Fallstown.

"You do know we've been set up? By your
daughter, no less."

He glanced at her, then away. "I'm not stupid."

"You don't need to get testy on me. Why are
you going along with it? Sunday's your day off,
your only day to spend with Amanda. And I ordinarily drive myself to the jetport and leave my car
in the long-term lot. It's no big deal."

Russ reached for the radio dial and silenced
the easy-listening station she'd selected. He'd
hoped a couple of hours in the car with Tory
would provide the opportunity to talk out a few
things. She hadn't cooperated. For the best part of
the drive, when she'd spoken at all, she kept the
conversation on Amanda and the pageant, with
occasional forays into her job, which she seemed
to enjoy even though it meant traveling so much.

Hell, why kid himself? She loved her job. And
she loved all this flying around to different places.
Spending time away from home. She could live
anywhere. She'd said at least three times that so
much travel was one of the pluses of working for
her company.

Stick to the plan, he lectured himself.

He kept his gaze on the exit ramp, a long, slow
circle that brought them out just down the road

from the Maine Mall. "My theory is that Amanda intended all along to back out of coming with us. She probably thinks if she gives us enough time alone together, something romantic will develop. I'm not so sure she's wrong."

That got Tory's attention. He heard her shift in her seat so that she could look directly at him.

The light changed and he made his turn. Ahead, he could see a plane taking off in the early-morning drizzle. "I'm aware Amanda is doing the matchmaker thing. Probably Beva still is too. But for a change, the idea doesn't irritate me. I find your company too enjoyable."

She had just enough sass to keep from being predictable. And right at that moment she was speechless, something he rarely saw and thoroughly enjoyed witnessing.

The silence didn't last long. They were on the airport access road when she spoke. "You're saying you've changed your mind about a personal relationship?"

"I'm saying I'm not so unwilling anymore." He pulled into the short-term parking lot.

"You picked a heck of a time to tell me something like that. How am I supposed to respond?"

Hiding his smile, Russ spotted a space and pulled in. That had been the plan. Keep her off balance until she tumbled right into his arms. He got out of the car and went around to the trunk for her luggage.

"Wait a minute," Tory yelped.

The delay while she unfastened her seat belt and collected her briefcase and purse kept her from reaching him before he had one of her suitcases in each hand and was heading toward the terminal. She trailed after him, still sputtering.

"Slow down, dammit. Have you taken into account that I may not have changed *my* mind?"

"Certain evidence indicates otherwise."

"Don't get cocky. One kiss doesn't prove a thing."

He found it illuminating that her mind went immediately to that kiss. Hiding a pleased smile he knew would only irritate her to see, he waited for her to go through the terminal doors ahead of him, then followed her down the stairs to the check-in area.

He had not been referring to their one intimate encounter, but rather to the way she'd been behaving around his daughter, the way she pitched in to help out in the store when things got busy, the hundred and one things about her that spoke to him without Tory having to open her mouth.

Somehow, in the short time since they'd met as adults, he'd become obsessed with Victoria MacDougall Grenville.

Was it foolish to hope they might have a chance at happiness? This trip to Houston was proof enough that their lifestyles didn't exactly mesh. But for the short term? Yes, he very much thought they had something to explore. He didn't just want her for his daughter anymore.

Probably never had.

He waited patiently while she completed her business at the ticket counter and checked the two pieces of matching, soft-sided luggage he'd carried in from the car. Even when she was irritated, she looked beautiful to him. She had on that silk blouse he liked, the one with the high neck and long sleeves that left so much to his imagination.

Once, Russ might have been daunted by the cool sophistication of her businesslike outfits, but now that he suspected most of her "don't mess with me" attitude was a facade, he was simply intrigued. The woman hiding behind the mask of a high-powered saleswoman was far more interesting than any other female he'd ever met.

"Maybe my timing is lousy," he admitted when she rejoined him and they began the trek upstairs, "but I wanted you to know how I felt before you left. You've become important to me, Tory, and not just because of all the help you've given Amanda."

At the top of the escalator a doughnut shop beckoned on one side, but Tory headed straight for the security checkpoint on the other.

"Your timing isn't just lousy, it stinks." She pointed to the sign that said TICKETED PASSENGERS ONLY BEYOND THIS POINT.

"Oh." He hadn't known he couldn't wait with her at the gate. He thought he'd been bluffing pretty well for someone who'd never flown. Because his parents drove back and forth when they visited from the South, he'd never even been to an airport before.

Suddenly uncertain what to do next, Russ just stood there, feeling awkward and out of place.

"Oh, for heaven's sake," Tory said. "Everyone knows they don't pay any attention to that." She hauled him into the line of people waiting to be scanned by airport security.

No one questioned his presence as they passed through the metal detector, but since he didn't know he was supposed to remove the coins and keys from his pockets, the alarm sounded. Loudly.

A few embarrassing minutes later, thoroughly deflated, he joined Tory on the other side of the gate. The airport security people had been very nice, he thought, but he felt like a first-class jerk. And Tory must realize now what a hayseed he was.

She didn't seem to. She *was* smiling, but it was a good-humored grin, not a sneer.

"I guess I should be flattered to see you so rattled," she said, grabbing his arm and steering him toward the waiting area for her flight to Cincinnati. She'd change planes there for Houston.

Grateful as he was for Tory's reaction, being in the airport was making Russ increasingly edgy. How could so many people casually watch planes take off and land? He deliberately chose a chair facing away from the huge terminal windows.

Tory sat next to him, but this no longer

seemed the time or the place for what he'd intended to say next. What was the point? No matter what he told her, she was still going to leave.

It wasn't as if he'd planned to declare his undying love, he thought glumly. He just wanted to change their relationship a little. To include the possibility of—why beat around the bush?—adding sex to it.

He cleared his throat.

Tory spoke before he could. "I'm a little nervous," she confided.

"Why?" She didn't look it. The phrase *cool as a cucumber* could have been coined to describe Tory Grenville.

First she shrugged. Then she admitted the terrible truth. "I know it's silly, but it's the flying. As much of it as I do, I still get nervous waiting in the terminal beforehand. I mean, does anyone really understand what keeps these foolish airplanes up in the air?"

Russ smiled as a surge of relief swept through him. Maybe they weren't so far apart after all.

"Well?" She was the one who sounded testy now. "How can an object weighing thousands of pounds possibly get off the ground?"

He squeezed her hand, offering comfort. "Simple," he told her. "It's magic."

Magic, Tory thought a short time later as her plane taxied into position for takeoff. That pretty much summed things up. Not only why planes flew, but also what she felt whenever she was in Russ Tandy's presence.

They'd never finished the relationship discussion he'd tried to start. She was just as happy they hadn't. *You're important to me* had been as far as she wanted to take things right now.

Sighing, she closed her eyes and tried to pretend she was on a bus. She'd be fine once they were in the air and she couldn't see anything below but clouds, but she hated takeoffs. The same sort of vertigo she'd felt looking out the back window at Tandy's Music and Gifts and down, down, down into Waycross Stream, afflicted her every time she caught a glimpse of the ground dropping away.

She wasn't too fond of landings either.

Think about something else.

At once her mind skipped to Russ, to the low-key, pleasant week just past, during which she'd spent more than a few hours at the music store.

She had reason to know just how little time Russ had alone with his daughter. He worked long days. Arranging to spend every spare moment with Amanda took some doing.

Tory approved, but at the same time she understood that Russ had told her the simple truth that day in his kitchen. His schedule did not allow for extras—like a woman in his life.

For that reason, his declarations in the car and in the airport had come out of the blue.

Her own reaction had not.

Tory sighed. Helping Amanda prepare for the pageant had been an excuse. She might as well admit it. Russ was the person she wanted to be with. His presence there had drawn her to Tandy's Music and Gifts day after day.

She'd been hanging around him like a kid at a candy store. All week long she'd clung to a false sense of security, feeling at ease in his company because there was no possibility of being completely alone with him for more than a few minutes.

With that as a given, they'd been free to talk about nothing . . . and everything.

Almost everything.

Apparently he enjoyed her company as much as she did his. She should have guessed what he was leading up to when he'd tried to teach her to pick out tunes on a practice chanter.

The beginnings of hope stirred deep within her. Tory was leery of counting on too much, but she thought that maybe, just maybe, it might be worthwhile to explore the possibility of a more intimate relationship.

She knew she'd never been this strongly attracted to anyone. Had she missed something during her marriage?

Maybe, she decided, she owed it to herself to find out.

The plane leveled out. She retrieved her briefcase, determined to get some work done.

But when she returned, Russ Tandy had better watch out!

Well before Tory got back home, her plans suffered a setback. At the sight of Beva waiting in the arrivals lounge on Thursday, she wanted nothing more than to unburden herself to her friend, but she could hardly go into detail with Jolene's ears flapping in the backseat of the car.

She had to wait until first thing Friday morning. As soon as school was in session and Jolene was safely out of the way, Tory knocked at Beva's kitchen door.

"Why am I not surprised to see you?" Beva greeted her. "Shut up, Kasey," she yelled at the dog, a border collie who'd come racing out at the first hint of company.

From the smell, fresh coffee was brewing in the kitchen. Beva, Tory knew, would have just seen her husband off on the commute to Three Cities. Her hair-cutting hours didn't commence until ten and ended at two. There was no point in working for herself, Beva always said, if she couldn't set her schedule to suit herself.

As usual, Beva's own coiffure was a disaster. She had a habit of running her hands through her short hair, leaving oddly shaped clumps behind. She rarely noticed. She was not one to care about appearance. She'd told Tory that she knew she was homely and had learned to live with it. What she didn't realize was that her open nature made her more appealing, spikes of dull brown hair standing on end and all, than most traditionally pretty women. Her husband flat out adored her. Russ admired her tremendously . . . and doted on her coffee.

"So what happened in Houston?" Beva asked as soon as they were settled at the table with two fresh cups of the steaming brew.

For a moment, being in Beva's old-fashioned kitchen reminded Tory of a similar scene in Russ's house twelve days earlier. An involuntary sigh escaped her. All the optimism she'd felt at the beginning of her trip had vanished soon after she reached company headquarters.

"I thought this was going to be a training and troubleshooting session," she told her friend. "Instead there was news. Big news. We're facing a merger."

"Which means?"

"Another company wants to buy the one I work for. If they succeed, things will change."

"Are you in danger of losing your job?"

"Not exactly. I have a good record. But this other company has a policy that discourages home offices. If the merger goes through, I'll be expected to relocate. To come into the office to work when I'm not on the road."

"Long commute to Houston," Beva said.

"I'd have to move out of Waycross Springs. Give up my house." She'd miss both, but even more she'd miss Russ and his daughter. Ever since she'd heard the rumors of what lay ahead, Tory had been shaken by the depth of her sense of loss.

"Nothing's happened yet," Beva reminded her.

"Not with the job, or with Russ," Tory muttered. Then, appalled, she stared across the table at her friend. She hadn't meant to say that out loud.

Beva grinned at her. "Sure you have those priorities straight?"

"Oh, yes. A job provides security. A man does not."

News of the changing job situation had altered Tory's thinking about Russ. She wasn't sure what was going to happen, but the potential for a move, soon, seemed a darned good reason not to deepen their relationship.

It was going to be hard enough leaving him as it was.

"He doesn't even know I'm back yet," she said aloud.

A small part of her was disappointed that he hadn't remembered when she was due to come home. She hadn't expected a shower of candy and flowers on her return, but she'd anticipated—dreaded?—a telephone call.

"Yeah, he does," Beva corrected her. "Amanda was over here for a while last night and Jolene told her we'd picked you up right on schedule. I'm sure Amanda's passed that news on to her father by now. And reminded him for the umpteenth time that the pageant is less than a month away. That story on her came out in the paper while you were gone. Jolene has been muttering darkly ever since, but I get the impression that Amanda herself has adjusted to being in the limelight. She actually seems to be enjoying the attention."

For once, Tory did not leap at the chance to substitute talk about the pageant for a discussion of her personal life. "What's the point of starting something that will go nowhere?" she asked.

"Don't know, hon. But if I remember right, you've got a date with the man next week. You may postpone the inevitable for a few days, but you'll have to face him then."

"Does everyone in town know I agreed to go out with him?"

A foolish question, Tory thought. Of course they did. That had been the whole point back when she'd said she would attend the small-business-association dinner with him. He'd asked her to help him get the matchmakers off his back by pretending to be his date.

"Maybe I'll come down with the flu," she muttered.

"Oh, no. You can't back out. You gave your word. And besides, if you don't show up, everyone will hear about it, and that will create all kinds of gossip. You may be able to escape by moving away, but Russ has to live here."

She *had* promised. And she *did* want to see Russ again, in spite of the danger to her heart.

"I'll go," she said, "but as a friend only."

She'd keep things cool and platonic.

Beva was able to mimic Tory's voice and body language perfectly. " 'I'll go, but I won't have any fun.' " Then, herself again, she shook her head in disbelief. "Friends? Good luck."

Tory sipped her coffee in a vain attempt to hide from Beva's too knowing gaze.

No, *platonic* wasn't how she felt when she was with Russ. For one thing, the oxygen level always seemed to diminish when he was in the same room. Or the same car. He gave the illusion of taking up all the space, of crowding her.

An illusion. That was all these feelings for each other could be. She told herself she had to remember that. She had to.

"That's the way it is, Beva."

"Will you listen to yourself? This is classic 'cut off the nose to spite the face' talk. Picking a job over a man! Honestly! Things are never that simple. And did you ever stop to think that Russ Tandy might be a career opportunity all his own?"

"He's not looking for a partner in his business, or for someone to marry. And why would I want to take on a man with a child anyway?"

"Hot sex?"

"I am not having sex with him!"

She felt her face color. She and Russ *had* been engaging in hot sex on a regular basis for weeks now—in her dreams. At night, her inhibitions gone, she became the sort of woman who could handle a fling. Even revel in one.

"It just can't work out for us," she told Beva. And, sadly, she believed it.

Throughout the week after Tory's return to Waycross Springs, Russ never once saw her in person. She did call, to tell him she was home and that she had brought a great deal of work back with her. She'd made time for Amanda, but she'd asked that the girl come to her house and had pointedly avoided inviting him. Every time Russ arrived to pick up his daughter, Amanda was always ready to go. Tory never gave him a chance to get out of his car.

Tonight would be different. She'd made him a promise she would keep. He'd arranged to have both Beva and Amanda remind her of it.

"This isn't a date," was the first thing she said when she opened her front door to him. She was already wearing her coat.

It felt like a date to him, but he didn't correct her.

"You look great," he said instead. He ushered her down the walk and held open the car door so that she could slide into the passenger seat. "I've missed you," he added, and shut her in before she could reply.

Keep it light, he reminded himself. All he'd

told her at the airport was that she'd become important to him, and that little bit had apparently scared her off. She'd probably go ballistic if he admitted he thought he was falling in love with her.

"I may have to move to Houston," she blurted.

He felt as if he'd been kicked in the gut. Silently, he let fly a few choice expletives.

Tory's statement certainly put a different slant on things. Now he understood her silence since her return. She was leery of starting something with him because she might be leaving soon.

But something had already *been* started. For him, there was no going back.

"May?" he asked.

"Nothing's definite yet."

"Then there's no sense in worrying about it until it happens, is there?" He kept his eyes on the street ahead, as if he didn't want to miss his turn. The truth was, he could have driven the route blindfolded.

This changed things for her, he thought. Or did it? Perhaps there had never been a chance for anything between them beyond the casual. Had he been deceived by his own wishful thinking?

He'd been confident earlier that he knew how this evening would end. Now he wasn't so sure.

Oh, he still hoped it would conclude the same way. He wanted Tory in his bed. But he no longer kidded himself that something permanent would be certain to develop afterward. What had seemed, while she was away, to have potential for a deep and lasting relationship, now appeared likely to be no more than a brief romantic fling.

Another quick glance at Tory showed him lips turned down in a frown as she stared through the windshield. He cursed the fact that they had so little time to discuss the bombshell she'd just dropped. Their destination was barely five hundred yards beyond the next intersection.

They approached the Sinclair House from the south, its least panoramic side, but from any angle the grand old hotel was impressive. Russ pulled in beneath the portico and handed his keys to the uniformed parking valet.

"Evening, Mr. Tandy," the young man greeted him. He ran his admiring gaze over the exterior of the car. The dark blue Intrepid still gleamed from an afternoon trip through the Wash 'n' Wax. "I'll treat it like it was my own."

Russ chuckled good-naturedly, even though he didn't feel much like laughing. "I've seen that wreck you drive, Kenny. Let's keep treating this one like *I* own it."

Inside, divested of their coats, Russ took Tory's arm to lead her through the huge, ornate lobby to the more intimate Fireside Room, where predinner cocktails were being served.

They'd talk later, he promised himself. For now, they had to socialize and pretend they were having fun.

At least a dozen people called out greetings the moment Russ and Tory appeared in the doorway.

Without warning, Tory's fingers tightened on his sleeve.

"Problem?" he whispered.

"I feel as if I've fallen down a rabbit hole and landed on that old television series *Cheers*. Everyone knows your name."

"A lot of these people recognize you, as well." Or at least they'd heard she was coming with him that night.

"Where are name tags when you really need them?"

She was the only one who did, he realized. Everyone else knew all their fellow businesspeople and their spouses. And probably the names of their kids and grandkids as well.

"Don't worry," he told her. "I'll prompt you on IDs."

She pasted a smile on her face and continued to cling to his arm. "I can get through this." She sounded as if she was giving herself a pep talk rather than speaking to him. "I am an expert at faking interest in social small talk."

Before his eyes, she changed, putting on what he'd begun to think of as her mask. She was suddenly all business, protected by a shell of artificial sophistication. It hadn't occurred to him until now to wonder what made her retreat behind it, nor had he realized how much being shut out bothered him.

Instead of leading her farther into the room, he steered her toward a window alcove where they could have a moment's privacy. "Don't hide from me, Tory," he said in a low voice.

"I don't know what you mean."

But she did. He could see it in her eyes. He wanted to understand, struggled to piece together the contradictory facets of her character, but he couldn't do it without her help.

At last she spoke. "I've had to learn how to cope," she said quietly.

"Cope with what?"

"Shyness. Paralyzing shyness. The kind that leaves a person speechless and unable to function. The only way I can manage is to will myself to become this . . . alter ego. This person who isn't afraid to speak up, who actually enjoys socializing. I was horribly shy until I went away to college. I still revert to that state when I'm faced with a situation in which I don't feel confident."

"So you turn yourself into superwoman instead?"

She smiled, as he'd hoped she would. He wasn't belittling her accomplishment. What she said made a lot of sense to him, but he didn't like seeing that business persona take over the softer, gentler woman he knew her to be.

"I still feel awkward and shy inside," she confessed. "Almost all the time."

"Why on earth did you go into sales?" he asked. It seemed the last job she'd want, feeling the way she did.

"To challenge myself. And you know what? I realized I love it. Love the traveling, meeting new people."

"Because you don't have to see them again?" he guessed.

Her startled look told him he'd hit the nail on the head. "I never thought of it quite that way, but I suppose you're right. They only see one side of me. I don't have to keep up this front all the time."

"And what do I see?" he asked.

"More of me than anyone else ever has," she said quietly.

They were interrupted then by their old music teacher, Mrs. Benning, but Russ felt he and Tory had made a connection in those few minutes alone. He thought he understood her a little better. He knew he wanted to deepen that knowledge.

"That's Lucas Sinclair and his new wife, Corrie," Russ said, keeping his promise to point people out to her. "Corrie and Tory," he added. "You two should start a vaudeville act."

"I'd expect a crack like that from a man who named his only child Mandy Tandy."

He winced. "An oversight. She was named after Melody's mother, who calls herself Amie. What we'd done didn't hit us until several days after the name was down on the official birth certificate. But you'll notice that I always call her Amanda."

Since Tory seemed herself again, they began to circulate, listening more than talking. The topics of conversation ranged from tourism, real and projected, to speculation about a recent shoot-out between an armed felon and the police. A state trooper had been slightly wounded.

"I apparently missed hearing about that while I hibernated at home over the weekend," Tory said. "Your brother wasn't involved, was he?"

"Not that I know of. He doesn't talk much about his job."

She made a face at him. "I think you'd know if he'd been shot at."

Russ shrugged, his attention drawn to the doorway of the Fireside Room. Two men had just come in, and Russ wasn't the only one dismayed by their appearance. Lucas Sinclair got a thunderous look on his face the moment he recognized one of the men as Stanley Kelvin, owner of the Phoenix Inn.

"Is that old feud still going on?" Tory asked. Kelvin's mother had been a Mead, and the Meads and the Sinclairs had been at odds for generations.

"Apparently." Russ's attention shifted to the other man. Roger Hillary.

So did Tory's. Then she looked up at Russ beseechingly and moved even closer to his side. "Do

me a favor? Find us a table for dinner without
room enough for Roger to join us?"

"My pleasure." Russ's relief was dispropor-
tionate to the situation, but he didn't stop to question why. He was just pleased to have won the
confidence, if not the heart, of the fair lady.
Through dinner, at least, she was his.

"Soon after I returned to Waycross Springs, I
agreed to meet Roger for a drink at the Phoenix,"
she confided as they continued to circulate. "We
were friends in high school, a couple of nerds who
were always on the fringes socially. Back then, we
spent time together just to have someone to hang
out with. I don't know what happened to Roger in
the years since, but I didn't care for the result. I
definitely regretted letting him escort me home."

"Why?" His stomach clenching in primal reaction, Russ waited for her reply.

Her tone was dry. "Maybe you remember an
expression we used when we were teenagers—
Russian hands and Roman fingers? That's Roger
to a tee." She again moved even closer to Russ
when she realized Hillary was watching them.

Russ immediately took advantage, sliding his
arm around her waist in a blatantly possessive way.
She let him get away with it. In fact, he suspected
that if she were honest with herself she'd admit
she enjoyed the sensation.

Maybe he wouldn't have to beat ol' Roger to a
pulp after all.

SEVEN

They sat with the Sinclairs and the Scotts at dinner.

"I understand you're newlyweds," Tory said to her host and hostess.

"We were married last May," Corrie told her. "Here at the Sinclair House. Out in the grove. It's not the most beautiful spot at this time of year, or during mud season, but in late spring it's gorgeous, and when the snow comes, it will be spectacular too."

A vivid image of a wedding formed in Russ's mind. His own wedding. His and Tory's.

"Have you wintered here yet?" Tory asked, blissfully unaware of her escort's thoughts. "I'm sorry. If we went to school together or something, I don't remember. I barely remember Lucas, since he's a couple of years older than Russ and I are."

Russ and I. He liked the sound of that.

"I came here last Christmas on a holiday," Corrie said, "and somehow I just never got around to leaving."

"She fell under the enchantment of the place," Lucas said, and the two of them exchanged one of those special smiles only couples who are very much in love can share.

Dinner was followed by several brief speeches, the presentation of a few awards, and announcements about the next business meeting. It was not yet nine when Russ and Tory left the Sinclair House. Country hours.

"Amanda will be expecting you," Tory said.

"No. She's staying at Beva's with Jolene tonight. A sleep-over."

Russ let the word hang in the crisp November air as they waited for Kenny to bring the car around. He wasn't sure himself if he was issuing an invitation or just making conversation.

"I should go home," Tory said.

He obliged by driving to her house. They didn't say another word to each other the whole way, and by the time he pulled up to the curb, her silence was grating on his nerves.

"I don't think it would be a good idea for you to come in," she said in that husky, sexy voice that drove him crazy.

"I'm not an out-of-control teenager, Tory. Nor am I a dirty-old-man-in-training like Roger Hillary. You say stop, I stop. But it makes no sense to deny that—"

"Stop right now." She turned to face him, memories of the last time they'd been in this situation showing clearly in her eyes. "Say good night, Russ. Let's stay friends."

"If that's what you really want."

He didn't believe it was, not for a moment. What she really wanted to do was kiss him again. She wanted to do far more than that. He could recognize his own longing in those enchanting almond-shaped eyes.

"What's the problem here, Tory? Level with me. Okay?"

"The problem is that part of me wants you to come in with me and the hell with what the neighbors will say in the morning when they notice that your car has been here all night."

"I can drive home and walk back," he offered.

"How . . . chivalrous."

Forcing a laugh, he got out and walked around to the passenger side in time to hand her out onto the sidewalk. All the way to her door, he kept her fingers tucked into the crook of his arm.

"Simple friendship is best," she said. She had her key out.

He took it and unlocked the door. "Only one problem," he told her. "You've gotten to me, Tory. I can't stop thinking about you. Or about what it would be like to make love to you."

Her sigh was deep. Sad. Full of regret. "I think about it too," she admitted. "I won't deny I'm tempted, Russ. But not here. Not tonight. Maybe never."

He chose to believe she was leaving the possibilities open, and as much as he wanted her, he knew he had to let her go. For now. He went no farther into her house than the front hall. He placed her key on the half-moon table, then turned to cup her face in both of his hands.

"Somewhere. Sometime," he promised. Utter conviction laced the soft words. "This isn't going to go away, Tory. It's too strong. Too pervasive. You've crept into every corner of my life."

"It can't lead anywhere," she said.

"All good things come to an end. Does that mean they should never begin?"

He left her then, forcing himself to end their evening without sharing the parting kiss they both longed for. "Another old saying comes to mind," he said as he walked out the door. "Seize the day." He didn't look back to see if she'd heard him.

"Seize the day."

The next morning, Tory couldn't get those words out of her head. Repeated over and over again in Russ's deep, slightly gravelly voice, they were driving her nuts.

She couldn't concentrate on her work. She thought about Russ all the time. And the night before, when she'd finally gotten to bed, she'd dreamed of him.

Graphic, detailed, erotic dreams.

"Maybe," she said to Pat, when the black-and-white cat leaped into her lap to nuzzle at her clenched fist, "I should just go ahead and find out if there's something to that business about dealing with sex by doing it. You know—get it out of my system."

Pat gave her an affronted look and hopped down again, stalking off with tail in the air, a picture of feline indignation.

"A lot you know," Tory called after her. "You were fixed when you were six months old."

Pat did not deign to answer that rude comment.

Sighing softly, Tory brooded a short while longer, then decided to make herself a calming cup of herbal tea. She knew what was at the root of her restlessness. Last night, when Russ had brought her home, she'd expected him to follow her inside. She'd hoped he would, in spite of her token protest.

Although it went against everything she thought she'd believed about herself, Tory had secretly longed for Russ to take the decision out of her hands, to overwhelm her with his kisses, to convince her to do something foolish, something wonderful. For once in her life she'd wanted to be ravished.

How disgusting.

How appalling!

How . . . tempting.

It wasn't, she realized, that she wanted to be carried off by some stranger. It was only with Russ that she had this fantasy, and only Russ she'd ever accept in real life as the "savage Scot" or "lawless pirate" or "rogue knight" or "splendid barbarian."

The list went on and on. Cliché after cliché. Very retro, and revealing entirely too much about Tory's deepest, darkest fantasies.

And of course she wouldn't truly be unwilling. She'd be his equal in desire, in passion.

Yeah. Right.

Stick to daydreams, she warned herself. Life was neither a soap opera nor an epic motion picture. Reality was apt to be one big disappointment.

The reality was that Russ didn't fit the profile of bad-boy rebel. He hadn't been one in high school. A bit of a hell-raiser on occasion, but all in all a good kid. And now he was, for the most part, a conservative businessman and responsible father.

Go ahead, an inner voice taunted. *Convince yourself he's dead boring*.

Another sigh escaped her as she sipped her own blend of ginger, peppermint, and chamomile tea. She really did have to decide what she wanted. Last night, Russ had told her things she'd have killed to hear him say way back when. True, he hadn't suggested anything permanent, and she'd have to be an idiot even to think of quitting her job on the off chance that the relationship might work out that way between them, but why had she been so afraid to take what he was offering?

She was a mature adult female, a successful businesswoman. Surely she could handle an affair.

The teacup rattled as she replaced it on the saucer. Right. Apparently she couldn't even think the word *affair* without suffering an attack of nerves. What was wrong with her, anyway?

The answer came with blinding clarity. Chad Grenville, her ex-husband.

Not that the fault was entirely his. She'd allowed him to exert too much influence over her thinking, while he had never given two cents for her feelings.

Damn Chad anyway! He'd left her plagued by insecurities about her own sexuality.

And damn her, for letting him get away with it.

Wasn't it about time she stopped letting his hang-ups influence her life, her decisions? So what if she was on the rebound? Maybe that was exactly what the rebound was all about.

And who better than Russ Tandy to . . . bound with?

He was a gentle man. A kind man. A considerate man. She could trust him not to hurt her. He could help her rebuild her self-confidence.

The only real risk would be to her heart. Somehow, she'd have to avoid falling in love with him. Then, when she left for Houston, if in fact she did have to move, it would be a painful parting but not an emotionally devastating one. They'd have explored the passion between them. She'd probably be ready to move on.

This logic appealed to Tory. All she needed now was the courage to act upon it. Unable to imagine coming right out and telling Russ she'd changed her mind, she concluded that she'd have to wait until he made the next move.

Her heart lurched in anticipation and she laughed aloud, startling both cats.

It never occurred to her that more than a week might pass before she even saw him again.

"This is a circus," Russ said as he surveyed the crowd gathered for the pageant's "training session."

Circus? he repeated silently. Try madhouse. The presence of over a hundred beauty-pageant contestants all in one place was overwhelming, even if the oldest *was* only sixteen.

Every one of them, and their mothers, seemed to be talking at the same time. Dozens of different hairsprays and perfumes, most of them too cloying for Russ's taste, scented the air. A blinding rainbow of colors, from jewel tones to palest pastels, deliberately eye-catching, adorned the hopefuls. Unfortunately, with so much to look at, one's vision blurred. Russ doubted the pageant judges, old hands at such displays, would be in the least impressed.

"You didn't have to come," Tory reminded him.

She wore a simple business suit and smelled of Ivory soap and herbal shampoo. To him that combination was far more erotic than any exotic floral essence or chemically enhanced designer aroma.

"Playing chauffeur for you and Amanda seemed like a good idea at the time," he answered.

That morning, at literally the last minute, he'd informed her that he would be taking them to Portland. He'd made arrangements to do so well in advance, of course, since taking a Saturday off wasn't that easy to manage. He'd counted on the fact that Tory wouldn't try to back out. After all, Amanda still needed her assistance. She shouldn't even be suspicious. Russ was just relieving her of having to drive and saving her the necessity of spending a night away from home.

The sudden change in plans had unnerved her, though. Russ smiled to himself as he recalled her first sputtered protests. Had she figured it out yet? he wondered. Probably not, since she'd already reminded him twice to cancel the room he'd previously booked for her and Amanda.

The "training session" was about to begin in the second-floor ballroom of the Carstairs Hotel, an old brick edifice in downtown Portland. This huge chamber opened out onto a mezzanine overlooking the lobby. At Tory's urging, she and Russ retreated in that direction. There the air was marginally fresher and the noise level dropped to something approximating a popular restaurant during the lunch-hour rush rather than a football stadium at halftime.

"She won't even notice if you take off for a while," Tory said.

"I'd know."

"Well, at least don't hover."

Was that pity he'd heard in her voice? "I don't hover." He was, however, the only father present. In fact, aside from pageant personnel and employees of the hotel, he was the only male anywhere in sight.

"You do so hover. Probably the only criticism anyone will ever level at your parenting, Russ, is that you're overprotective. Amanda's not a baby anymore. You have to learn to let her handle things by herself."

"I'm not leaving her here alone." *Unprotected.*

"No, you're not. That's why you recruited me. I'll stay here. You can go somewhere else. Take a walk around the Old Port. See the sights or something."

"Shop? Stop at a bar?" Gentle mockery laced his suggestions.

He was staying put, and not just to keep an eye on Amanda. Nothing, not even being surrounded by scores of screeching females, was going to stop him from spending the day with Tory.

Her exasperation amused him, and he almost

laughed aloud when she literally threw up her hands and gave in.

"Have it your way," she said, "but please notice that Amanda is having a wonderful time. Don't you dare rain on her parade."

Because he had never seen his daughter quite so animated, Russ agreed. In the course of the next hour he had to swallow rude comments more than once, but he still managed to force a smile when, during a break, Amanda came bouncing toward them from the ballroom. Following more slowly after her was another girl.

"This is Summer Sapienski," Amanda announced. "She's been in about a zillion pageants."

Summer appeared to be several years older than Amanda. Tall and slender, almost skinny, she was pretty enough, but to Russ's critical gaze she appeared to be all show and no substance. Her vapid expression and loose-limbed movements made him think of a puppet.

An overblown strawberry blonde hove into view, a clipboard clasped to her chest and a militant light in her eyes. At first Russ thought she must have some official connection to the pageant, but after a moment he realized she was Summer's mother. She went by the improbable name of Red.

"And you're sweet little Amanda's parents," she gushed after she'd introduced herself.

Neither Russ nor Tory corrected her. In fact, Tory took a step closer to him. The smile that had felt frozen in place on his face eased and became genuine.

When a pageant official called for all the girls to gather around again, Red expelled a blissful breath. "Isn't she just darling?"

She was not talking about Amanda.

Cynically, Russ studied young Summer, who in turn seemed to be assessing the competition. She had a cold, calculating look in her eyes, much like the one on her mother's face. A quick glance at Red's clipboard revealed that she'd been jotting down nasty little comments about the shortcomings of each contestant in her daughter's division.

A few minutes later, when Red sailed off to accost Ms. Arsenica, both Russ and Tory let out sighs of relief. "Good grief," he muttered. "What a dragon."

"Be careful what you say in front of Amanda," Tory warned. "She took a moment to whisper to me that she thinks her new friend Summer is 'way cool.' "

"Heaven help us." These days, those words were Amanda's highest accolade. She'd used them, he remembered, to describe the gown she and Tory had selected.

"Let it ride," Tory said. "She's a smart kid. She'll see through the phoniness sooner if you don't try to warn her."

He mimed zipping his lips but continued to keep a close eye on his daughter.

"Why didn't you correct Mrs. Sapienski when she thought I was Amanda's mother?" Tory asked.

"Why didn't you?"

"Maybe I felt I needed a protector."

He liked the sound of that.

Tory was silent for a moment, then sent a smile his way that made his blood heat and his palms sweat.

He'd deliberately left Tory alone for eight long days. Putting pressure on her, he'd reasoned, would do no good. Such tactics worked no better on grown-up ladies than they did on little girls. Besides, he couldn't have spent any substantial amount of time alone with her during the week, even if she'd been willing.

This evening was different. They'd have two solid hours, when Amanda was attending the "get-acquainted party," to spend as they pleased. For that stretch, they'd have no nosy neighbors to worry about.

All he had to do was survive the remaining hour of this training session.

And get Tory to agree to accompany him to the hotel room he had not canceled.

"Why can't they just be themselves?" he grumbled after watching girl after girl parade across the small stage at one end of the ballroom. Every one of them attempted a variation of that odd, slouchy walk affected by high-fashion models. The Sapienski girl had it down perfectly, and clearly Amanda was trying to imitate her new friend.

"Let her play at being super model," Tory said, reading his thoughts with uncanny accuracy. "It's only for today and next weekend. Amanda will be your little girl again before you know it."

"Can't be soon enough for me." And would she really ever be his little girl again? he wondered. "How can you be so nonchalant about all this?"

"Amanda isn't my daughter. I don't have twelve years of taking care of her to color my sentiments."

"Ever think about having kids?" he heard himself ask.

Tory was careful not to look at him. "No. This gig as chaperon is as close as I want to come."

"You're more than a chaperon."

"Mentor, then."

Mother figure, he thought. Foster mother. Stepmother. Only for Tory to be Amanda's stepmother he'd have to be thinking about—

Marriage?

His first instinct was to reject the idea. He'd told himself when Melody left that he'd never again be interested in any woman on a permanent basis. To commit himself to a lifetime with someone just to obtain a new mother for Amanda had struck him as a bad idea. Still did. Unless that someone could be Tory.

Tory, who might be moving soon, he reminded himself.

Tory, who'd just said she'd never thought about having kids and had implied she didn't want the responsibility of a family.

Tory, who was the best thing to come into his life in years.

Keeping her there, talking her into marrying him, had definite appeal. Russ felt a rueful smile settle on his mouth. He wasn't even sure Tory would agree to deepen their one-on-one relationship. To make love with him. It was a long way from there to becoming a family.

But that didn't mean he wouldn't try to convince her both were terrific ideas.

By the time Amanda joined them for the supper break, she was in high spirits. "This is so much fun!" she told them enthusiastically. "Everyone is soooo nice."

Once again Tory caught his eye and shook her head, warning him not to do or say anything to diminish Amanda's delight.

Didn't want kids, huh? he thought. Nope. He wasn't buying that story. She was much too good at mothering. Far better than Melody had been.

He got more proof of it just a few minutes later when they were leaving the ballroom. Tory noticed a solitary figure in the shadows and stopped.

"There's a girl sitting on the steps leading to

the stage," she whispered. "She looks as if she's been abandoned."

Amanda followed the direction of her gaze. "That's Lisa Delacroix. Her mother dropped her off at the beginning of the training session and went to meet her boyfriend. She won't be back for Lisa until after the party."

"What's the kid supposed to do in the meantime?" Russ asked, outraged that any parent could treat a child so callously. Not surprised, of course. Melody had done far worse. But he was furious at the injustice, just the same. Some people didn't deserve to have children.

Amanda shrugged, but Tory was already walking over to the girl. A few minutes later she returned. "She says Florence—I assume that's her mother—expects her to shift for herself. But good old Florence didn't leave Lisa any money with which to buy a meal and there isn't anyone here to look after her until the party starts. I've asked her to come to supper with us."

Russ approved. Amanda looked doubtful, but didn't object. It turned out the two girls were the same age, which meant they were in direct competition with each other.

By the end of the meal, however, they were chattering happily together. They returned to the Carstairs Hotel arm in arm and still talking a mile a minute. Neither of them noticed another pair of contestants half-hidden in the shadows at the corner of the building, but Russ caught sight of a distinctive glow and stopped to take a closer look.

Neither of the girls sneaking a smoke was old enough to buy cigarettes legally. One of them looked no older than Amanda and Lisa. The other was Summer Sapienski. While he could understand the girl's need to defy her domineering mother, this sure wasn't the best way to assert her independence.

Just thinking about the warped relationship the mother and daughter must have, left a bad taste in Russ's mouth. Once again he longed to caution Amanda about the company she was keeping. Tory's earlier warnings were all that kept him silent as Amanda headed for her get-acquainted party.

Tory was right. He did tend to be overprotective.

If he'd done a good job raising Amanda, he told himself, then his daughter already knew right from wrong. He had to have faith that she would not be foolish enough to smoke, no matter how "cool" the other kids might claim it was.

"So, what do we do to kill time while they're socializing?" Tory asked.

"Want to hang out with Red and the other mothers?"

Tory's answer was a mock shudder of horror.

"Well, then, how about you and I spend some quality time together? I missed you this past week."

"I missed you too," she confessed, but he sensed a reluctance in the words.

Taking her elbow, Russ steered Tory toward the elevator. He was looking forward to being completely alone with her, even if that situation didn't develop into anything physical. If she said "no dice" right out, he could abide by her decision. He'd regret the necessity, but he'd yield to her wishes.

"Remember what we said once," he asked, "about putting all the cards on the table and being honest with each other?"

"Yes."

She was definitely wary now, and resisted getting into the elevator with him until he shifted his grip to her hand and tugged, then caught her shoulders to hold her there while the elevator doors slid closed behind them.

They were alone.

"What I honestly want is you, and I think you're equally attracted to me."

She looked slightly stunned.

As the elevator rose he held her at arm's length, his eyes boring into hers. Beneath his hands, he felt her tremble. Nerves? Fear? Passion? "If I'm reading you wrong, if you still don't want anything but friendship between us, tell me now."

"You're not wrong." She sounded breathless.

"Good." His own breathing had gotten pretty erratic too. "I lied to you earlier," he confessed, fishing in his pocket for the key card and pressing it into her hand just as the elevator doors opened on the top floor. "I didn't cancel the hotel room."

Tory looked away, overwhelmed by the intensity of Russ's gaze. An empty hotel corridor stretched ahead of them. She had only to step out of the elevator, walk a little way down the hall, use the key Russ had just handed her, and close out the rest of the world.

She felt as if someone else had taken possession of her body. Her legs moved, her feet took one stride, then another. Her arm lifted, aiming the card at the slot. Moving like an automaton, she entered the hotel room and let the door close behind them.

The click as it automatically locked sounded like a gunshot in the silence. It galvanized Russ into action.

All unnatural, mechanical sensations ceased the moment he took her in his arms. She knew exactly what she was doing, and why.

Desire surged through her, into her most private parts, setting off a tingling and a throbbing such as she'd never experienced before. She did not simply yield to his kisses and caresses, she invited them, returned them, reached eagerly for greater intimacies.

"This is crazy," she whispered.

"Yes."

"Impulsive."

"Yes."

"There's no future in it."

"Probably not."

Probably. She clung to that word. Nothing was absolute. There was always the slight chance that all her dreams could come true.

The room was illuminated only by the light filtering in through one floor-to-ceiling bay window overlooking the Old Port. It was enough. They could see to locate the queen-size four-poster bed.

"Slow down," he whispered, and she felt him smile against her throat. "I want to savor you, savor this."

"I don't think I've ever been savored before."

"No? Then you've had only fools make love with you."

"Fool," she corrected before she could stop herself.

For just a second he hesitated. Then he was kissing her again, sliding his big, gentle hands down her back and using his grip on her hips to lever her closer.

He felt very large, and for the first time a quiver of trepidation raced through her. Attuned to her every reaction, Russ loosened his hold. Their bodies were still in contact, still perfectly aligned, but she no longer felt quite so overwhelmed.

"I won't hurt you, Tory."

"I know." And she did. But she was still nervous.

She liked kissing him. She liked touching him. But what if she froze up? What if she couldn't satisfy him? What if he rejected her efforts to please him? Worse, what if he taunted her with her inadequacies, as Chad had done?

No. Not Russ.

She lifted her hands to his face and smoothed her fingertips over the slight hint of stubble on his jaw. She trusted him to take good care of her, physically and emotionally. He might not love her, but he did care. They had become friends during the last few weeks, friends who'd been potential lovers all along.

"Tory? You okay with this?"

She answered him with her body, moving close again.

Close? She suddenly wanted to crawl inside him. Her seeking lips found his mouth. Her tongue surged inside, claiming him as he began to strip away both their clothing and her inhibitions.

By the time they were naked together and he had donned a condom, she had no more doubts, no more hesitation. The slip and slide of their bodies did nothing but excite her.

Friction, she thought. That's all it was. His parts against hers. And yet it felt like so much more. The physical sensations were augmented by shivers of pure emotion.

She was, she realized with a sense of bemused amazement, having *fun*.

And then she could no longer think at all.

She stopped trying to analyze what she was feeling, stopped trying to separate one sensation from another.

Instead, she let him absorb her wholly. Devour her, even as she devoured and absorbed and savored him.

He was a caring, skillful lover. Every touch was a revelation. He played her like one of the instruments in his shop, until she sang a song of pure ecstasy, and only then did he enter her and reach for his own release.

They tumbled back to earth slowly, the fall cushioned by soft clouds. It was almost a surprise to discover they were lying among the pillows of an ordinary bed.

"Mmm," Tory murmured. "Nice."

For the first time in her life she understood what all the fuss was about. She *had* missed out on something in her marriage, something she'd found with Russ. Not just the physical sensations, either, but a sense of rightness, of closeness.

A low chuckle rumbled near her ear. "Only nice? I thought it rated higher than that. Try spectacular."

She'd been right about that too. He did have a voice perfectly suited to being heard in the dark across a shared pillow.

"It was rather wonderful," she agreed.

Wonderful . . . and scary.

She knew for certain now that her plan to get those sexual urges out of her system by giving in to them had backfired. Once was not going to be enough!

A lifetime might not be enough.

To her delight, Russ rolled toward her and propped himself up on one elbow to gaze down at her. His eyes were slumberous, filled with affection and something darker, a reflection of her own sudden fierce sense of—dare she think it?—possessiveness.

Not a politically correct sentiment, perhaps, but honest.

"I'd like to keep you here forever," he murmured.

With one hand, he traced the curve of her hip and waist, then cupped her breast, admiring it in a way that made her think he saw it as a work of art. Oh, the man was good for her ego!

"I feel the same way." She dared touch him in return, and was rewarded by a very masculine sound of pleasure.

Suddenly she wanted all she could have of him, now, no matter what might happen in the future. A flicker of doubt cast a momentary shadow over her happiness. This *was* temporary. It had to be. She'd be a fool to let herself get too involved with Russ and an even bigger one to fall in love with him.

Then Russ began to kiss her in earnest and she

shoved such considerations firmly aside. She could no longer focus on anything but him. She'd think about the future later, she told herself as she surrendered to the magic.

Much later.

EIGHT

"We have about ten minutes before we have to meet Amanda," Russ said as he began to dress. Meet Amanda, then drive all the way back to Waycross Springs with her in the backseat. "I wish my daughter were younger," he added.

"So she would never have gotten the idea to enter this beauty pageant?" Tory asked.

"So she'd take a nap on the way home and we could say whatever we felt like saying without fear of being overheard."

"Don't kid yourself." Tory's voice was muffled as she hunted through the tumbled bedclothes for her slip. "Even little pitchers have big ears."

"Let's just hope she doesn't have any big suspicions." Or big expectations, he added silently.

Fully clothed, his hair finger-combed, he turned to watch Tory as she put herself back together. What expectations did she have? Had he been nothing more than a means to fulfill a fantasy, to satisfy her curiosity? Or did this brief, passionate interlude mean as much to her as it did to him?

He tried not to anticipate her, wanted to deny he had any hopes himself, but his deepest yearnings had rushed to the fore the moment he'd discovered the sheer rapture of possessing Tory Grenville. He wanted more. More time with her. More of her generous gift of her body. More of her in his life . . . and Amanda's.

Ordinarily, he was not a greedy man, but now he was guilty of that sin. He'd developed a sense of possessiveness about this woman.

One night would never be enough, he thought as he watched Tory button her blouse. He sensed it was too soon to speak of permanence, though. Instead he searched for a compliment to pay her, to let her know at least a part of what he felt.

"Before I met you, I never realized how sensual silk could be," he said. "Makes a man think about buying sheets in that fabric, just to try them out."

"Yes, well, clothes make the man, or the woman. So they say." A nervous laugh underscored her abrupt mood swing and put Russ on red alert.

Either he was out of practice giving compliments, or she had little experience receiving them. He'd always thought of himself as a perceptive person, except where Melody had been concerned, but he suspected he was missing something now.

Tory fumbled with the remaining buttons, more clumsy than he'd ever seen her. She was acting as if she couldn't wait to get away from him and yet he was certain their enjoyment had been mutual.

Maybe he shouldn't have brought up Amanda. Hardly romantic to talk about his daughter right after making love. And Tory *was* under the impression that she wasn't mother material.

Then an alternative possibility struck him. Hit him like a wallop upside the head with a baseball bat, actually. She wasn't used to this. She'd been married, but she'd never had a lover, never met a man in a hotel room, never behaved like an abandoned woman . . . till now.

Unable to subdue the grin forming on his face, Russ closed the distance between them. He was her first, maybe in more ways than one. When he remembered her little squeak of surprise as her climax hit, his lips stretched to their limit. She'd hinted earlier that her ex-husband hadn't been much of a human being. Apparently he hadn't been very considerate in bed either.

Which meant the logical reason why she was suddenly acting as nervous as the proverbial cat was insecurity. She'd taken a big risk with him, and as perfect as the last two hours had been, second thoughts and doubts were both natural and inevitable. She needed reassurance, not only about the rightness of what had passed between them, but also about her performance.

"You are one in a million, Tory," he said.

Her head snapped up. Panic flashed in her eyes. "You aren't going to use the L-word, are you?"

His grin abruptly turned into a frown. "Not if you don't want to hear it."

He wanted to tell her how special she was, how much he'd cherished the moments they'd stolen together. She'd responded to him beautifully. But he realized now that she hadn't once said how she felt about him.

What did he want her to say? After that L-word crack, he could hardly present her with a declaration of love or expect one in return. And yet, he was 99 percent sure that love was exactly the emotion he was feeling.

Both of them had said that word before, to other people. They'd both heard it said in return. And they'd both been deceived.

"I would like to . . . see you again," he said instead.

If he was in love with her, if it was real, it would last. He could afford to give Tory time to come to grips with her feelings for him.

At the moment she was uncomfortable about what had already happened. Tension knotted the muscles in her neck and arms as she bent to put on her shoes. When she straightened, a mask had dropped into place to conceal her thoughts.

"We have a lot to do," she said. "Only a week left."

She was talking about the damned pageant!

The transformation in her was startling. His soft, yielding lover had abruptly taken on a brusque, businesslike persona, becoming a woman who was, at best, a mere friend of the family.

Russ stared. Which was the real Tory? The hard shell he saw now, the crisp voice that was enumerating all the tasks that remained to be done between now and the pageant, were enough to make him doubt the conclusions he'd just reached.

Hell, for all he knew, Tory had affairs all the time! Insecure? In need of reassurance? Not the woman who stood before him now. This female seemed utterly self-confident, completely in control of her emotions . . . if she even had emotions.

Great sex sure could scramble a man's brains.

"We have plenty of reason to see each other until the pageant is over," she finished.

She might be speaking of getting together for tea and crumpets, but he knew she meant she'd welcome him into her bed as well as her kitchen. For the next week.

"And beyond that?"

The veneer cracked, just a little, just for a moment. He saw the flash of panic in her eyes again before she gave herself a shake and forced a social smile. At least that break in her composure told him one thing. She wasn't as calm about planning an affair with him as she wanted him to think she was. She employed this facade, this distancing, as a means of self-preservation. It was that shyness she'd told him about. He should have known.

Any doubts about her character dissipated as rapidly as they'd emerged. Tory was not two-faced or deceitful, as Melody had been, but rather a woman trying very hard not to let herself become vulnerable.

She didn't yet trust him not to hurt her.

Russ could understand that and, understanding, was able to curb his impatience. He'd met the real woman beneath this surface poise. Given the chance, he'd coax her out again.

"Let's take one thing at a time," he suggested.

"Fair enough."

He had a great many things he wanted to say, but not now, not when they had to collect Amanda and head home. Fragile as his present relationship with Tory was, he could not risk speaking impulsively. Too much was at stake.

He'd wait until he was sure she was prepared to listen, until he felt she'd be inclined to accept that what he felt for her was real. At that time, he hoped, she'd be able to admit she returned his love. For now, however, he'd have to put up with her defense mechanisms.

She seemed to want to pretend nothing significant had just happened between them. He resigned himself to letting her act as if they'd never let all the barriers down, never been naked and sweaty together, sharing the most fantastic lovemaking he'd ever known.

She gave him a bright, brittle smile. "Brace yourself to spend the next few hours listening to your daughter enthusiastically recount every detail of her evening's excitement. She's going to want to share it with us."

"I'm braced."

And very glad that Amanda would be so preoccupied with recounting her own adventures that she wouldn't be likely to ask her father how he'd spent the evening.

When Tory breezed out of the hotel room ahead of him, perfectly put together, no longer appearing to be in the least frazzled or upset, he considered the possibility that he'd just hallucinated their entire passionate interlude.

No, he decided. It had been real. So were his feelings. He'd honor her wishes and avoid speaking of love, but he wasn't forgetting a thing.

And in the course of the next week, he intended to become as much a habit with her as teatime was to an Englishman.

A week later, at the pageant rehearsal, Tory had to work hard to keep her attention on the contestants. This time the ballroom was at the Sinclair House on the second floor. Again it was a huge room with a bandstand at one end. On that small stage stood eleven of the twenty-three girls in Amanda's division, Miss Preteen.

Tory gave Amanda a thumbs-up sign, but her thoughts strayed to Russ as they had, day and night, for most of the last week. During that time she'd frequently seen him in person. They'd made love on almost every occasion they met, in stolen moments when Amanda was in school and Mrs. Ruthven was minding the store.

Each time it just got better. That was the problem. Tory was very much afraid she was addicted to Russ Tandy's brand of lovemaking.

She didn't have a clue how he felt. She knew she satisfied him physically, but he never said anything about what he thought of her, or where he believed their relationship might be headed.

Her own fault, she supposed. She'd been the one to warn him against saying he loved her. She'd been so afraid, that first time, that he would feel obliged to say the words. She'd wanted to hear them only if he meant them.

Their omission probably meant he did not love her even a little. What else was she supposed to conclude?

"What brand of hair dye do you use to get that color?" Red Sapienski asked, breaking into Tory's reverie. Red still clutched the clipboard, making Tory wonder if it was permanently attached.

"Excuse me?"

"Hair dye? What shade for Amanda's hair? I'd

like to try something similar on Summer next year."

Tory was too startled by the idea of a mother dyeing her young teenager's hair to do more than sputter a denial that Amanda's hair color was anything but natural.

"Fine. Be that way." Glaring, Red took herself off to annoy someone else.

Tory's attention returned to Amanda, who had just come off the stage. Summer was with her, whispering something in her ear. Advice, Tory supposed, and felt uneasy.

After rehearsal was over, during the walk to Russ's house, Tory asked what Summer had said.

"There's a question section in the pageant," Amanda explained. "Each division has a separate one. The answer we give makes a big difference in whether we make the semifinals or not."

"Do you know what your question will be?"

Amanda nodded. "What has been the most significant event in your life?"

"So what's your answer?"

"Well, I was going to say that it was last January, during the big ice storm when the power was out for such a long time that even people who had their own woodstoves or generators were beginning to need help. Daddy and I volunteered at the shelter the town set up. They let me help cook, and it was kind of fun. And I helped with the animals too."

"Animals?"

"Emergency shelters won't let people bring their pets, but here in Waycross Springs we set up a shelter for the animals, too, in the building next to the people shelter. They needed volunteers to walk the dogs and clean the cages and all. I helped. So did a lot of other kids from my school."

"That sounds like a fine answer."

But Amanda was shaking her head. "Summer says it'd take too long to explain, and that I've got my priorities all wrong."

"Oh?" Tory didn't like the sound of that. Neither did she believe Summer was the sort of girl to offer to help someone out of the goodness of her heart. Whatever her reasons for befriending Amanda, she had an agenda. Tory could only hope Summer was motivated by nothing more harmful than the desire to create a cadre of devoted fans for herself.

"She says I should say something to flatter the judges, like telling them that the most important thing that ever happened to me was being accepted to compete in this pageant."

That advice fit Tory's worst opinion of Summer Sapienski and led her to go against her better judgment and offer Amanda some advice of her own.

"Don't you think that's a little shallow?" she asked.

"Well . . . yeah. But Summer is way cool and she says—"

"Amanda. Think. Wouldn't the judges want you to be yourself?"

The girl looked doubtful.

Oh, great! Tory thought. The pageant was making Amanda cynical. *Meet new friends, build self-esteem, develop self-confidence, develop skills needed to succeed in the workplace*, the promoters had trumpeted in their literature.

Sadly, lying might indeed be one of those skills. Tory couldn't deny she'd seen people get ahead in the business world through deceit and deception. Rumor had it that politicians weren't always truthful either.

"It's up to you," Tory said, "but I think the judges expect you to answer the question honestly. I know your father does."

"Hang in there," Tory whispered into Russ's left ear.

The break before the "formal wear" section of the pageant was just about over. Tory had made a quick trip backstage to help Amanda change clothes, as she had earlier between the "casual wear" and "talent" portions of the Miss Special Smile competition.

As Russ tried to get comfortable in a folding chair much too small for a man of his height, he reminded himself that this torture could not go on much longer. They'd already survived the first two rounds, each composed of one hundred and fifteen contestants in five categories, from the Shirley Temple moppet stage, with one little girl actually sporting ringlets and a crinoline under her skirt, to five very mature young ladies at the "Ms." level.

Most of them, he'd quickly realized, had little talent, especially those who presented musical numbers. But few of them lacked self-confidence. A couple of the girls who sang had been every bit as loud as Amanda's bagpipes.

To Russ's right sat his brother. Gordon glanced pointedly at his watch and looked relieved. "I've got to go," he said. "My shift starts in less than an hour."

"Lucky dog," Russ muttered.

The vacated seat was immediately filled by their cousin Susan, who'd been across the aisle with her two daughters. "My girls are jealous," she told him in a stage whisper they could probably hear in New Hampshire. "They're already lobbying to enter next year's competition. Do you think Amanda will do this again?"

"God, I hope not!" Russ sent a fervent prayer winging heavenward. Once was enough.

"I didn't realize you had so much family in Waycross Springs," Tory said when Susan was distracted by a question from Daphne, her youngest. Also in the audience were at least ten other members of the Tandy clan.

Recognizing a note of strain in the question, Russ gave her a sharp look. "That bothers you?"

"Just makes me wonder why you didn't ask one of your cousins or your aunts to chaperon Amanda."

"There are lots of Tandys in town," he said carefully, "but we hardly ever see them except at Thanksgiving and Christmas. Amanda isn't all that close to any of them."

"They seem to have turned out for the pageant."

He shrugged. "Might be family loyalty. Might be them checking up on me to report to my folks in the next long-distance phone call. Doesn't matter. For Amanda's sake, I'm glad of the show of solidarity."

"Jolene is here too." Tory sounded pleased but puzzled by that fact.

The lights lowered and the next segment began. Finally, they got to the "question" portion of the show. Almost every girl in Amanda's division said the most significant event in her life had been learning she'd been accepted to participate in this pageant. One girl varied the pattern a bit by saying it was getting into her first pageant. Since she didn't look any older than Amanda, Russ had to wonder how early she'd started . . . and whose idea it had really been. Another young lady caused a small ripple of amusement when she identified the most significant event in her life as "being born."

"Do you know what Amanda's going to say?" Russ asked Tory.

"I hope so."

He let it go at that, keeping his attention on his daughter as she was called to the microphone. He had to admit that the green dress looked beautiful on her. His heart swelled with pride as he saw her start to use that slouchy model's walk, then switch to her own natural, bouncy step. By the time she was halfway through her explanation of their volunteer work at the emergency shelter, there were tears in his eyes. Unashamed, he let them fall.

He felt Tory's fingers grip his hand. "You've got a winner there," she whispered.

"I know."

It didn't matter at all to him that his daughter was not chosen as a semifinalist in the Miss Special Smile competition.

"She was robbed," Susan declared. Since the pageant was over as far as she was concerned, she heaved herself out of the chair and headed for the exit, her daughters with her.

Families of other girls who hadn't made the cut were departing as well, though the exodus wasn't wholesale. With ten semifinalists in each division except "Ms.," where all five girls automatically became not only semifinalists, but finalists, there were still forty-five contestants left. They all seemed to have cheering sections in the audience.

"We'd better find Amanda," Tory said. "I don't know how she's going to react to this. When

I last saw her, she was certain she was going to make the finals." A wry smile flickered and was quickly gone. "Heck, she was sure she was going to win. She asked me if I wanted to go to the national competition in Florida with her."

"How was she supposed to get there?" Russ asked, startled. This was the first he'd heard about any national competition.

"The winner of this pageant gets her airfare and hotel room paid for. Of course the folks who go with her have to pay their own way."

"I'm glad she didn't win," Russ said.

Tory couldn't help but hear the heartfelt gratitude in his remark and sent him an odd look.

"I wouldn't have begrudged her the expense," he said. "It's the flying part that rattles me."

"You've never flown, have you?"

"Nope. I was uneasy about you traveling to Houston by air. I'd be hard-pressed to risk my only child on a plane. The idea of going with her doesn't bear thinking about." He looked for some sign that Tory thought less of him after his confession, but found no censure in her eyes.

"You're going to have to learn to believe in magic," she told him, then led the way to the lounge the Sinclairs had set aside as a changing room. "I'll go in and get her. You wait here for us."

They took a long time, even considering that Amanda had to change out of the floor-length gown. He hoped she wasn't in tears in there.

Russ walked the length of the hall and started back again, automatically checking the rear entrance to the lounge in the process. He didn't really think Amanda would try to sneak out the back way, no matter how upset she was or how much she might want to avoid facing him in defeat, but when he did spot someone leaving the room, he stopped and stared.

It was not Amanda. It was Jolene. Moving in a manner that could only be called furtive, Beva's daughter crept away from the door, then scurried off without noticing Russ. Odd, he thought. He was certain she'd been in there consoling her best friend. Surely even a budding feminist should be allowed to do that much.

"Daddy," Amanda called.

All thought of Jolene vanished. Prepared to be sympathetic, Russ hurried toward his daughter. Amanda was too still, and looked much too solemn for a twelve-year-old. Her bounce was missing. When he was close enough, she flung herself into his arms.

The hug helped both of them.

Afterward, he lifted her chin with one hand. "I'm proud of you, Amanda."

"I didn't win." Her voice broke. "I really wanted to be Miss Special Smile."

"Hey, honey, you're *my* Miss Special Smile. Don't you know that? Come on, give me a sample."

Her effort was halfhearted, but at least she

didn't dissolve into tears. He couldn't have handled that.

It wasn't until they were leaving the hotel that he noticed Tory was trailing behind, as if reluctant to join their family circle. As if she wasn't certain she'd be welcome.

"Am I missing something?" he asked when the three of them were in his car. He'd parked on the street this time, avoiding the valet parking.

"It's nothing," Tory said, but her voice trembled almost as much as Amanda's had earlier.

From the backseat, Amanda mumbled, "You weren't supposed to hear what I said."

"Hear what?" Russ asked.

Amanda clammed up.

"Tory?"

Silence emanated from the passenger seat.

"Someone better tell me what's going on. The tension in this car is thick enough to cut with a knife."

"I accidentally overheard something Amanda said to Jolene."

"And that was?"

More silence.

Pulling teeth, he thought. Neither one of the women in his life was cooperating worth a damn. Giving up on Tory, who obviously wasn't going to rat on Amanda, he turned in the seat and fixed his daughter with a steely stare.

"Spit it out, Amanda. We're going to sit here

in the car until you do." For emphasis he hit the button that locked all the doors.

"I said she gave me bad advice. I wouldn't have been cut from the semifinals if I hadn't listened to her."

"What bad advice?" Russ asked.

"Be yourself," Tory told him. "Apparently, I was wrong. Honesty wasn't what the judges were looking for."

"I should have answered my question differently."

Amanda was pouting now. He could see her in the rearview mirror even after he turned around and shoved the key in the ignition. It was not a pretty sight.

"I should have said it was getting accepted by the pageant, just like everyone else did."

Russ started to speak, but Tory's hand on his arm stopped him with a silent plea to let Amanda work this through for herself. She wasn't ready to listen to reason.

A stricken look still lingered in Tory's eyes. She cared very much what Amanda thought of her, he realized, and his daughter's words had hurt her deeply.

"We'll talk about this again." Russ started the engine. "All three of us."

There had to be more to Amanda's uncharacteristic attempt to cast blame than simple disappointment over losing a competition. Unless she was more Melody's child than he'd thought.

He quickly rejected that notion. Like flying, it did not bear thinking about. Unfortunately, he couldn't put his finger on just what it was that made him so certain Amanda wasn't telling them the whole story.

Or why he feared Amanda's behavior boded ill for his future with Tory.

NINE

"Things are strained," Tory admitted.

"Obviously," Beva said, "or you wouldn't be celebrating Turkey Day with us."

Tory sat at the kitchen table while her hostess basted the bird in the oven. Dinner was still an hour or more away, giving them time to talk.

Only the day before, Tory and Russ had agreed they'd better not try to spend the Thanksgiving holiday together, though they'd been planning to do so. Inexplicable as it seemed to them both, Amanda's attitude toward Tory had continued to deteriorate after the pageant. She'd gone from whispering that Tory was responsible for her loss of the Miss Special Smile crown to loudly proclaiming that "fact" to anyone who would listen. The girl now seemed dead set against having anything to do with her former mentor, chaperon, and friend.

"I just don't understand what caused the turn-around," Tory said. "Amanda and I were getting along just fine until she was eliminated. I felt I knew her, which is why I have a hard time swallowing the idea that she's so shallow she has to have someone else to blame when things go wrong." She shook her head. "It makes no sense."

"She's the one who decided what answer to give," Beva said. "She made her father proud, even if she didn't impress the judges."

"Made him proud," Tory agreed, "and then made him very, very angry. She's put him in an intolerable position. I wouldn't be surprised if she asked him right out to choose between us."

No question about which one of them he had to pick. Russ's loyalty belonged to his daughter, which was as it should be. Tory was the outsider, the interloper.

"I think it's over," she said aloud.

"Has he said so?"

"Not yet, but it's just a matter of time." She sighed. "Still, for a . . . temporary thing, it was grand while it lasted."

Plunking herself down in the chair opposite Tory, Beva glowered at her friend. "Will you listen to yourself? This isn't like you, Tory. Giving up without a fight. Letting a mixed-up kid decide your whole future."

"My job will—"

"You don't know what's going to happen there yet. And I know you, pal. You were thinking

maybe there was something for you here. No."
She held up a hand, traffic-cop style. "Don't
bother to deny it. I saw the look on your face
when you came back from Portland."

That face now flushed, a furious wave of color
ending all hope Tory might have had of convinc-
ing Beva she'd jumped to the wrong conclusion.
She could hardly fault her friend for trying to give
her a pep talk, either. It was just that she'd started
to think that Amanda's attitude might be a bless-
ing in disguise. The break with Russ was all but
accomplished already. If she did have to move,
leaving could hardly get more painful.

"I thought the buyout talks had stalled," Beva
said.

"There could still be a hostile takeover."

"And you want to work for these people?"

Tory had to smile. "It isn't as bad as it sounds.
We aren't talking about the Old West here. No
shoot-outs. No bloodbaths." And since she'd
worked for the same company for many years, she
had seniority. Her accumulated benefits would
not be lost in the change of ownership, only her
choice about where she would live.

"So, if they say jump, you ask how high?"

"I do if I want to keep working." Beva's prob-
ing was annoying Tory, and some of that irritation
crept into her tone of voice.

For a time the two women sat in silence. Tory
inhaled the aromas of roasting turkey and freshly
baked bread. Without warning, those scents made

her long for a home of her own, a family of her own to cook for on special occasions.

How pitiful, she thought. Why was she feeling sorry for herself when she was here with friends? She got to share Beva's family, her husband, Nolan, and their daughter, and even the dog, Kasey. Surreptitiously, she wiped away a trace of moisture from the corner of one eye and pasted on a smile.

But when she looked across the table, she saw that Beva's attention had shifted away from her. The other woman's gaze was fixed on a spot behind Tory's head. She jumped a little when her friend barked out a command.

"Jolene Scott, stop eavesdropping and get in here this instant!"

Shamefaced, the girl crept into the kitchen, coming to a stop a few inches away from Tory's chair.

"How long have you been listening?" Beva demanded.

"Since Tory said things were strained."

It was a toss-up who was more embarrassed by the admission, Jolene or Tory. At least, Tory thought gratefully, she hadn't said anything specific about sleeping with Russ. Lord knew she and Beva had implied enough about what they'd been up to, though, and Jolene was sharp as a tack.

"You've been acting weird ever since Amanda entered that stupid pageant," Beva said. "I think the time has come to set the record straight.

What, exactly, were you two girls plotting on all those afternoons when you were supposed to be doing homework?"

After a good deal of shuffling from foot to foot and quick, wary glances at Tory, Jolene folded before her mother's implacable will and confessed. "Amanda feels the same way I do about beauty pageants," she whispered. "At least she used to, until Tory came along."

Startled, Tory had to bite her lip to keep from protesting aloud.

"When they sent us invitations to participate, we got this idea."

"Why do I have the feeling I won't like this?" Beva wondered aloud.

"Amanda's prettier than me, so we decided she should be the one to enter. We figured she was a shoo-in to win against all those big phonies."

Pretty is as pretty does, Tory thought.

"Let me guess," Beva said. "When she won, she was supposed to denounce beauty pageants as demeaning to women, et cetera et cetera." She made a circling motion with one hand.

Eyes wide, mouth all but hanging open, Jolene nodded. Amazing, Tory mused, how each generation thought it was the first to come up with an idea.

"So? What went wrong?"

At her mother's prompting, Jolene answered, but not before she again shot a covert glance in Tory's direction. "Amanda says Tory brainwashed her, made her think she really wanted to be a beauty queen. If she won, she wouldn't have said a thing, even though we had a whole speech written out. She'd just have accepted the crown and gone on to the nationals."

"Brainwashed," Tory repeated in astonishment. "By me?"

Jolene nodded. "That's what she said. She was explaining it to me when you came into the changing room. How you brainwashed her and then gave her bad advice." The girl paused, as if struck for the first time by the contradiction in Amanda's version of events.

" 'What a tangled web we weave,' " Beva quoted softly, " 'when first we practice to deceive.' "

"Ironic, isn't it?" Tory said. "All those lies and then her own honesty ended up costing Amanda the crown."

Jolene looked from one adult face to the other in confusion. "How come you aren't mad?" she finally asked Tory.

"I'm too busy feeling other things," Tory told her.

Sadness. Disillusionment. Why on earth hadn't Amanda just owned up to her change of heart? Why had she felt it necessary to find a scapegoat?

Tory knew she'd never encouraged Amanda to "betray" the elaborate scheme she and Jolene had concocted. She hadn't even known what Amanda's true goal was. That meant the pageant experience itself had seduced the girl into wanting to win for all the usual reasons. And when she had been cut, she'd been bitterly disappointed. Ashamed to admit that to Jolene, to explain her tears, she must have given her friend the first excuse that came to mind, casting blame on Tory.

And now she'd taken a stand. Backing down had to be one of the hardest things in the world for a person to do at any age. For a twelve-year-old? Next to impossible.

"You going to tell him?" Beva asked when Jolene had been banished to her room until dinner was ready.

"I can't rat on Amanda to Russ. She needs to be the one to explain this to him."

"Good luck talking her into that!"

"You convinced Jolene to own up."

"I'm her mother."

A few hours later, after Tory returned home, she tried phoning Amanda. She lucked out in that Russ's daughter was the one who answered the phone, but her success rate dropped off the chart the moment she attempted to reason with the girl.

Amanda listened in silence as Tory repeated Jolene's confession.

"I understand why you lied about your reasons for wanting to enter," Tory told her, "and I can see how participating changed your opinion of beauty-pageant contestants. I even understand that you were embarrassed to admit that to Jolene.

But this has gone far enough. The last lie you told, the one about me brainwashing you, is hurting everyone. You, me, and your father."

"You did tell me how to answer the question."

"I said you should be honest and I'm asking the same thing of you now."

Apparently she was asking too much.

"No way," Amanda said.

It was far too easy for Tory to put herself in Amanda's place. Plainly, the girl couldn't face her father's disappointment in her any more than she'd been able to deal with the possibility Jolene would be disillusioned because Amanda had betrayed their cause.

"Amanda," Tory pleaded, "your father—"

"You better not think you're going to marry him!" Amanda blurted out. "I won't let you. If you get married, you'll have a kid and I'll get stuck baby-sitting. That will *ruin* high school for me!"

With a resounding crash, Amanda hung up.

Tory stared at the phone. Where had *that* come from?

Family at Thanksgiving dinner? Probably. Amanda must have heard speculation about her father and Tory. People knew they'd been seeing each other. It was impossible to keep anything secret in a town the size of Waycross Springs.

Reaching down, she scooped up a passing cat, holding the squirming feline close for a moment before she let him go. A baby? With Russ?

For just a moment she let herself consider the

possibility. She could actually imagine having a child with him, something she'd never been able to envision with Chad.

That was not a good sign. Probably meant she'd gone and fallen in love with the man, in spite of all her good intentions.

Tory sighed. She'd do better to stick with pets, she thought. Animals were far easier to deal with than children.

Or lovers.

Russ did not like sneaking around.

He wanted his relationship with Tory to be out in the open.

That was why, on the Friday evening after Thanksgiving, he did not book a room at the Sinclair House. Instead he arranged to meet Tory for a drink in one of the hotel's lounges.

While he waited for her to arrive, he thought back on the previous night's bittersweet telephone conversation, when he'd had to report that Amanda didn't seem to be getting over her snit or calming down. She now appeared to resent and dislike Tory every bit as much as she had once welcomed her into their family circle as adviser and friend.

Russ didn't understand it at all, but he could not ignore Amanda's opposition to Tory. How could he love a woman his daughter despised? How could he consider asking her to marry him?

She was everything he wanted in a wife, he thought as she entered the room. Beautiful. Generous. Sexy as all get-out. She'd abandoned her usual business suits for a softer look, a dress of dark green wool that brought out the red in her hair.

A few minutes later they sat talking quietly over drinks.

"It's been almost a week since the pageant. I keep hoping she'll come around." Russ moved the ice around in his glass with the swizzle stick and stared into the amber liquid. It was the exact color of Tory's eyes.

"Amanda's confused," she said.

"About what? She could at least explain that much!"

Tory started to speak, then shook her head.

"Why do I get the feeling you're keeping something from me too?"

"Don't be silly."

She pasted on that false smile he loathed.

"Amanda just needs a little more time to work through whatever is bothering her. Trust me. I've been a preteen girl. Everything is traumatic at her age."

"There it is again," he said.

"What?" From the puzzled look in her eyes, Russ knew she truly didn't understand what he meant.

"You're closing yourself off, hiding your feelings behind that sophisticated, self-confident . . .

front. I hate it when you retreat there, Tory. There's no need of it, no need to hide. Not from me."

I love you.

He wished he could add those last three words aloud, but he knew she wasn't ready to hear them. Not yet.

Maybe never.

And as long as Amanda was so bitterly opposed to having Tory around, there was no way he could push for anything permanent between them.

"You do it too," she said thoughtfully.

"Do what?"

"Hide that way. Blank your expression. Pull into yourself. It's rather unnerving to witness."

"Tell me about it."

She sipped her rum and cola and regarded him solemnly over the rim of the glass. "You do it most often when someone mentions Melody. And you did it once in the store, when Amanda interrupted us. You'd been flirting with me. You were"—she lowered her voice—"aroused. Then . . . nothing. I guess we both had reasons to keep a shield in place."

"Not with each other. Not anymore." He held his breath, waiting anxiously for her response.

"No. Not with each other."

He exhaled, relief coursing through him. He could almost see the barriers come down as she reached for his hand across the table.

"In my case it's habit. Self-defense. You'll have to call me on it anytime you see me do it."

"Only if you'll return the favor. I don't have anything to hide. Not from you."

A wicked gleam came into her eyes, adding sparkle to the hazel depths. "Why am I suddenly visualizing us naked?"

Startled into a laugh, he squeezed the hand he now held. "Because we both hide behind clothes too. I've been thinking I should reconsider that business about a dress code at the store. Do you think customers are put off by my formality?"

"No need to go overboard." Tory's teasing tone and the look she was giving him made his breath back up in his throat.

She really was stripping him in her mind. That incredibly erotic notion got him hot and bothered in an instant. As his body hardened, his voice dropped to a lower register.

"Shall I tell you a secret?" he whispered. "I like you better in grubbies than in suits, except for one, or dresses. No pretense. No artifice. No business persona in old jeans and a baggy sweat-shirt."

"Thanks, I think. What's the one exception in suits?"

"Can't you guess?" He leaned in close and whispered the words *birthday suit* in her ear.

Tory's breath caught. Her cheeks flamed, delighting Russ.

"In that case," she said, "we're both way over-dressed."

They took a room at the Sinclair House after all.

Time had just run out for them, Tory thought as she read the fax sent by her office. What a way to start the week.

Maud worked on Monday mornings, so when Tory burst into the store, Russ took one look at her face and ushered her directly into his office. There they could have privacy.

"What's wrong?" he demanded as soon as he'd closed the door behind them.

"That buyout I told you about? The merger went through. If I want to keep my job, I have to move. Move or resign. There isn't much choice. I need to work to support myself."

For one desperate moment en route to the store, Tory had contemplated asking Russ to go with her, to pull up stakes and move to Houston. Talk about dreaming the impossible dream! He'd never abandon Waycross Springs.

She didn't want to leave either.

The prospect hurt more than she had ever imagined it could. In just a few months she'd begun to build a new life in her old stomping grounds, and not only in connection with Russ. She'd made friends, taken an interest in the community. She'd remembered how much she loved the smell of the fresh mountain air and the hint of frost in the morning and a thousand and one other tiny things.

This was home.

It was more than that to Russ. Waycross Springs was his whole life. He was the third-generation owner of a small business that was practically an institution in the town. She couldn't ask him to consider leaving even if Amanda weren't in the picture.

But Amanda was. Right at the center. And her aversion to Tory seemed to be as strong as ever. Saying anything to Russ about why Amanda was acting the way she was seemed as futile to Tory now as it had a few days earlier. Why upset the relationship between father and daughter when she was going to be leaving anyway?

Belatedly, Tory realized that Russ was just staring at her, his expression as blank as she'd ever seen it. She couldn't tell what he thought about her news.

React, dammit! she wanted to scream.

"When do you have to go?" he asked.

"They want me in place in Houston within the month." By the beginning of the new year.

Russ said nothing. He didn't beg her to stay. He didn't even meet her eyes.

She cleared her throat. "I'll miss you."

"Same here." But still he didn't suggest any alternatives.

If she was honest with herself, Tory would

have to admit there'd never been much chance of anything permanent developing between them. All her doubts resurfaced in a painful rush. With a rueful grimace she acknowledged there was still a lot of that skinny, shy, unpopular kid in her.

Russ turned away, reaching for the door.

This was it then. So long and thanks for all the—

The lock clicked loudly in the silence of his office.

"Russ?"

A dark and dangerous gleam in his eyes, nostrils flaring slightly to give him an almost feral look, he walked slowly toward her.

"If we haven't got a lot of time left," he said, loosening his tie, "then let's make every moment count."

A wild thrill swept through her. Tory's throat went dry, but her lips curved into a delighted, welcoming smile. "Am I about to be ravished?"

Words were not necessary. He answered her by discarding tie and jacket and civilized behavior. By the time he was close enough to touch her, her body was already prepared to welcome him. She reached for the buttons on her blouse, but before she could undo the first one, his hands clamped around her waist, lifting her onto the desk.

Her skirt slid up indecently, helped along when he shifted his grip to her thighs and moved them apart to create a space for himself. He stepped into the vee he had made, touching his body to hers. Tory nearly exploded right then and there.

She sucked in a tremulous breath and looked down at the place where their bodies met. His erection strained against the fabric of his slacks. Her skirt was hiked up so high that she could see the crotch of her panties. She could swear she was visibly throbbing.

A tremor shook her, making her grab hold of Russ for support. She lifted her eyes to meet his searing gaze and her breath deserted her once more. His pupils were so large, so black, that hardly any color could be seen.

For a moment they froze that way, staring into each other's eyes, their aroused bodies pulsing in unison. Then, very slowly, he began to undress her.

Hurry. Hurry, she wanted to scream. She knew he was as eager for completion as she was. But there was something so erotic, so compelling, about being teased and tormented this way that she could not find it in herself to rush him.

With great deliberation and shaking fingers, he peeled off the silk blouse and short skirt and dispensed with her camisole. He managed the panty hose with suspicious dexterity, leaving her sitting there, in broad daylight, on top of his desk, wearing nothing but a tiny pair of French-cut panties.

His clothing went next, and all the while he never broke eye contact. Only when he was gloriously naked did Tory shift her gaze. Her heart beat faster at the sight of him, so ready and so eager for her. As he sheathed himself to protect her she shimmied out of her panties in a rush, her appreciation, her desperation so obvious that it brought him to his knees in front of her.

"Oh!" she gasped as his hands once more clamped down on her thighs.

She was literally incapable of speech for the next few minutes. And when she would have screamed in release, he moved quickly, muffling the cry with lips that still tasted of her and sliding home just as the contractions of the most amazing orgasm she'd ever had were at their peak. The feel of his climax began a new spiral of pleasure, even better than what had gone before.

Limp and exhausted, they clung to each other, her head resting against his chest. Holding him tightly, breathing hard, she listened to his heart thud loudly beneath her ear.

Amazing.

"That certainly did make every moment count," she whispered when she could manage speech.

She felt a chuckle rumble through his torso. "I didn't want you to forget me."

"Don't worry about it. There's not a chance in the world that I ever will."

With one finger, he caught her chin and lifted it so that she had to meet his eyes. "This probably won't change anything," he told her, "but I think you should know that I love you."

She had to close her eyes for a moment. How could one sentence bring so much pleasure and so much pain? She was in deep emotional trouble here, for she knew exactly what Russ meant.

"I'm pretty sure I love you too," she admitted.

"Only pretty sure?"

Pull yourself together, Tory ordered silently. He was right. This didn't change a thing.

"Our timing stinks."

"Your job is taking you away." It wasn't a question.

"Yes."

She felt cold when he left her to dispose of the condom and collect their clothing.

"If you're hoping I'll offer you an alternative to moving to Houston, offer you marriage, I can't do it, Tory."

Not with Amanda so set against her. Tory understood. "I didn't expect you to. The timing's off for that too."

He gave a short, rueful bark of laughter. "No sensible woman would want to marry me anyway. Amanda's mother left me with a lot of emotional baggage."

I could help you unpack it. She squelched the thought before she could express it aloud. "If this is all we have," she said instead, "it's still pretty wonderful."

He deposited the garments, his and hers, on

the desk and gathered her close once more. Tory sighed and clung, cherishing every moment with him, no matter how bittersweet.

She'd gone into this with her eyes open. In the beginning she'd expected nothing more than a passionate affair. She could hardly complain if that was all she got.

"We still have a few weeks before I leave," she murmured. "What was it you advised a while back? Seize the day?"

He put enough space between them to give her a hard look, the heat in his gaze reminding her that they were both still naked. Then he grinned, an expression gleefully boyish and sinfully wicked at the same time.

"I'm open to suggestions," he said, "but you do realize that after this morning we can hardly go back to making love anyplace as mundane as a bed."

TEN

Russ's temper was still at a boil when he arrived at Tory's house with his daughter in tow. Bad enough that Amanda had entered the pageant under false pretenses, but she'd lied to him. All that business about wanting to win scholarships and gaining self-confidence. She'd behaved even more reprehensibly toward Tory, not only lying to her but lying about her.

"You will apologize," he said again as he rang the doorbell.

Every word of the phone call from Beva that morning still reverberated in Russ's mind. How she'd found out the truth he did not know, did not care. He was just glad she'd passed on what she'd learned to him.

The showdown with Amanda, which followed Beva's call, had not been pleasant. She'd pouted. She'd gotten teary-eyed. She'd accused Tory of ratting on her. But in the end she'd listened to what her father had to say and grudgingly agreed with him that if there was any blame involved in losing a competition fairly waged, it belonged squarely on her own shoulders.

Her mother had been good at shifting responsibility. Russ was taking no chances that Amanda would follow in Melody's footsteps.

The woman who opened the door at the Mac-Dougall house was the same Tory he'd first met weeks before—hair pulled back and held by a coated rubber band, no makeup, wearing ratty jeans and a baggy sweatshirt. His spirits lifted just at the sight of her.

Her smile at seeing him wavered when she caught sight of Amanda. His daughter was trying to make herself invisible behind him, but she was too big for that. Too grown up, he thought with a silent sigh of regret.

"This is a surprise." Her voice wary, her eyes more so, Tory stepped back to let them enter.

"Amanda has something to say to you."

Shifting from foot to foot, her gaze on the carpet, his daughter mumbled the words he'd told her he expected to hear. "I'm sorry, Tory. I shouldn't have told Jolene you brainwashed me. You didn't cause me to lose the competition. I chose what to say for myself."

Unfortunately, Amanda didn't sound as if she meant a word of it.

"Apology accepted." Tory's quick response

prevented Russ from intervening to demand more of his daughter. "I'm at sixes and sevens around here," she added, "but I think I could scare up some hot chocolate if you'd like a cup."

She led the two of them into the living room and kept going at a fast clip through the connecting dining room and into the kitchen. One cat—Dick, he thought—headed for the hills. The other, the big Maine coon, merely opened one eye, registered the presence of newcomers, and went back to sleep.

Amanda looked as if she wanted to bolt, too, enough in itself to make Russ insist they stay. "Think of it as drinking a toast or shaking hands to seal an agreement," he told her. "It's the polite thing to do and it probably won't kill you."

Heaving a long-suffering sigh, Amanda flounced across the room and flung herself down on the sofa. Only then did she seem to notice the packing boxes and the piles of tissue and all the doodads set out ready to be wrapped.

"What's going on?"

"Tory's moving to Houston." He thought he'd been braced to see concrete proof of her decision. He'd been wrong. A wrenching sense of emptiness settled over him as he looked around. "She'll be gone by the end of the year."

Deliberately, he chose a chair facing away from the array of packing material and ended up with a view of the sofa and the wall behind it. A rectangular area lighter than the surrounding wallpaper plainly showed where a picture had hung until recently. A landscape of a local scene, he recalled, done in watercolors. Tory had told him that her mother had painted it years ago and that it was one of her favorites.

So she was taking something of her roots with her.

And she was taking his heart.

Over the last two months she'd gradually become part of his life. In the last couple of weeks touching her had become as necessary to his survival as food and water. And in the last eight days, since the explosion of passion in his office . . .

No place as mundane as a bed, he'd said. It had been tempting to go for thrills, to make sure neither one of them ever forgot the other, but it turned out they didn't need kinky settings to make an indelible impression on each other. Beds had been just fine, and they'd been in both his and hers as often as they could manage it. The kinkiest they'd gotten was the time one of the cats had decided to climb onto Russ's back when he was on top of Tory, inside Tory. He'd been unable to dislodge the beast, and it had hung on for the ride. Russ and Tory had dissolved into gales of laughter afterward.

"Love me, love my cat," she'd sputtered, giggling.

Love me, love my daughter, he'd thought.

He couldn't imagine feeling so free with anyone else, ever. He thought she felt the same.

And there were things he still wanted to experience in her company. He'd like, just once, to spend an entire night with her. That was something they'd never been able to manage. They probably never would now. Time was getting short, and although her impending departure lent a sense of urgency to their passionate encounters, he'd gladly have done without that particular addition to the thrills.

One of Tory's lined tablets had been tossed onto the table next to the sofa. He picked it up and skimmed her neatly written list. Over half the items were ticked off, things she'd packed, things she'd stored. His fingers clenched on the pad as he read the rest.

house: sell or rent?
Christmas/farewell present: Beva
Christmas/farewell present: Russ
Christmas/farewell present: Amanda?

Smiling wryly, he tossed the pad aside. She'd erase the question mark after Amanda's name now, he supposed. Get his daughter something to remember her by. Then she'd go off to Texas and find new friends, new lovers.

"Daddy?"

He glanced up at the sound of Amanda's voice and was struck by the odd expression on her face. She looked almost sick with worry.

"Why is Tory leaving?" she asked.

"Why don't you ask her?" he suggested.

Tory returned a few minutes later. She carried a tray holding three steaming mugs of cocoa.

"What's going to happen to the cats?" Amanda asked when she'd blown on the hot chocolate to cool it and taken her first tentative sip.

Perched atop the china cabinet, where it could keep watch over the profusion of crates and cartons, one of them lazily swished its tail and peered down at them through slitted eyes.

"They go with me," Tory answered. "They're old hands at this. They've moved twice before."

She'd gotten custody, in other words. Tory might not care for mothering in the ordinary sense, Russ thought, but she treated those two fur balls as if they were the most precious of babies.

"On the plane?" Amanda sounded appalled.

"Well, I did think about that, only they'd have to fly as cargo. The airlines allow for one pet per flight in the passenger compartment, but they'd never go for two of them, even if I put them in the same carrier. They'd have to go in the hold and I'd have to sedate them. So, I'm going to drive to Texas instead."

"Do you think Pat and Dick will be happy living there?" Amanda asked.

What did she really want to know? Russ wondered. If Tory would be happy? He'd give a lot to hear the answer to that question himself.

Saying nothing, he watched the woman he loved drink her cocoa, listened to her chatter gaily about her job and the apartment a business associate had found for her and the warmer winter weather she was sure she'd enjoy once she got used to it.

Ask her to stay, his heart said.

Her happiness is more important than mine, his conscience countered.

Tory would be happy only if she had a fulfilling career. He couldn't offer her that.

Russ now had some hope that the rapport Amanda had once shared with Tory might be restored, but he had to face facts. Tory didn't want to be Amanda's mother. She didn't want to be anybody's mother.

He could not ask Tory to stay, to marry him. The last thing he and Amanda needed was another unhappy, bored wife and mother who'd up and leave them at some later date. It wasn't just his own heart at risk, he reminded himself. He had a daughter, a girl on the brink of womanhood. He couldn't take the chance that she'd form such a deep attachment to Tory that she'd end up being unbearably hurt.

Even though Tory was no Melody, no more than Amanda was her mother all over again, the legacy his late wife had left still haunted Russ. He didn't see that he had any options. He could not put what he wanted first. He had to put his daughter's well-being ahead of having Tory in his life.

Tory herself would applaud that decision.

"Russ?" Her worried, questioning voice snapped him back to the present. "You okay?"

He offered the first explanation that came to mind. "Sorry, I was thinking about the store. It's a real madhouse this time of year. Last-minute Christmas shopping from now till the twenty-fifth."

In actuality, these days the store held a lowly third place in his heart.

"I was just telling Amanda I'll be heading west before Christmas," Tory said. "It's a long drive to Texas."

What was he supposed to say to that? Her plans were made. He had no say in them. Yet when he looked at her, his heart was in his eyes, willing her to offer to stay, to try to work things out.

Fool, he chastised himself. It wasn't going to happen. He had to stop wishing for the impossible. He broke eye contact and stood. "I do have to get back to the store."

"There's something I'd like to arrange before I leave town," Tory said. "It's a Christmas present, but getting it requires your cooperation. Yours and Amanda's."

Christmas present? He knew what she really meant—"Christmas/farewell present."

But Russ found he couldn't deny her anything, even that. "You name it, you've got it," he promised.

❖━━━━━❖

"I don't know how you managed to talk me into this," Russ grumbled. Six days had passed since his hasty promise. He'd been trying to wriggle out of it ever since.

Tory shot an impish smile in his direction. She refused to give in to the blues. They were here in the mall at Three Cities, surrounded by Christmas shoppers. This was a happy time, dammit!

Music filled the air, bright and brash and promising wonderful things. The plans *she'd* made would be faced unafraid, all right. Unafraid and, sadly, alone.

She'd made another list. Checked it twice too. But it was a wish list in the true sense of the word. Some sort of job at the Sinclair House? Unlikely. Her own business in Waycross Springs? Highly speculative. Working for the state's tourism bureau? There *was* an opening, and she'd applied for it, but surely that was a long shot. Her plans were made. She couldn't live on hopes and dreams. Unless the man at her side gave her a solid reason to change her mind and stay, she'd be gone in less than a week.

She slanted a glance at Russ as they made their way through the merry throng toward a small shop at the end of the food court. With the colder weather he'd traded his leather coat for one of L.L. Bean's warden-style parkas. He'd unzipped it as soon as they came inside and now, as she watched in admiration, he shrugged out of it, drawing her gaze to his broad shoulders and lean, lanky build.

Her mouth went dry. She ought to be used to him by now. Just looking at him shouldn't send her into a tailspin.

When he glanced her way, she quickly pasted a smile on her face and gestured toward the store just ahead. "Here we are. At least pretend to be enthusiastic."

"Here" was Alexa Winterbottom's photography studio, the same one Tory, Beva, Jolene, and Amanda had visited at the end of the summer. She'd made an appointment for Russ and Amanda to pose for a photo together, her Christmas present to them. And to herself.

Alexa recognized Tory and Amanda at once. She was as eccentric in her dress as before. This time, in keeping with the season and capitalizing on her own rotund form, she'd dressed in a Santa suit. Minus the beard.

Tory explained what she had in mind. A family picture. A memento. Nothing fancy. Just real people posed nicely in their own clothing. Russ had worn a suit for the occasion. Amanda was in a dress.

"No makeup?" Alexa looked shocked. "No hairstylist?"

"We're going for the natural look, Alexa," Tory explained. From Russ's reaction to Amanda's earlier photos, she knew he wouldn't want her primped and painted.

Grumbling audibly, the fussy little photographer herded them toward the studio section of her shop. Christmassy background? She could do that. More than one person in the shot? No problem.

But when they were inside, Tory found herself being hustled into position on a low bench.

"Oh, no. Alexa, I'm not—"

Alexa talked right over her protests. "You're wearing green. This is good." She grabbed a bunch of fake holly and shoved it into Tory's hands like a bouquet, then pushed Russ down next to her on the bench. She arranged Amanda behind them, a hand on each of their shoulders, not letting anyone get a word in edgewise.

Tory expected either Russ or Amanda to object. Neither did. When she started to rise, Russ caught her arm.

"Stay."

Meeting his eyes, she froze. For just a moment she allowed herself to believe that he was asking for more than her cooperation in posing for a photograph.

The click of the camera brought her back to reality. She forced a smile and let Alexa have her way. Shot after shot followed. They were arranged and rearranged and constantly told to smile. Without a word of complaint, Alexa's three subjects followed orders.

And then it was over. They were in a closet-size room, staring at the computer screen on which Alexa displayed her first proofs. The photos came up in reverse order.

"I like this one." Amanda stopped the sequence somewhere in the middle of the poses.

Tory just stared. They looked so much like a family. Father. Daughter. Mother.

"I wish you weren't going to Texas," Amanda said. "I wish you could stay here with us."

Tory didn't dare look at Russ. "I thought you'd be glad to get rid of me," she finally managed to say. "That baby-sitting thing," she added in a softer voice, hoping Russ wouldn't catch the words.

"I changed my mind," Amanda said. "Last week, when I saw you'd been packing, I thought I'd driven you away and I was glad at first. And then I started thinking that maybe it wasn't such a good thing for you to go." She pointed to the picture still on the monitor. "Well, just look at us. We belong together. The three of us."

Tory's heart beat so loudly, she was sure Russ must be able to hear it. Her breath all but stopped as she wondered what he would say. If even Amanda could recognize that they had somehow *become* a family . . .

Russ said nothing. He depressed the key to continue viewing proofs, clicking slowly through them until the last photo, the first shot in the sequence, came up on the screen. Tory saw herself staring deeply into Russ's eyes, her own much wider than usual. Alexa had caught the exact moment when she'd dared hope they might have a future together.

"They say you can't hide from a camera," Russ murmured.

"Hide what?" The words came out breathy and much too soft.

"Love."

Hers for him? Or his for her? She looked again at the picture Alexa had taken. The answer was there, in their likenesses on the small screen. They loved each other.

"Will you marry me, Tory?" Russ turned toward her and took both her hands in his as he asked the question.

Did he really think there was any chance she wouldn't accept? Tory flung her arms around him. "Yes," she whispered. "Yes. Yes. Yes."

Their lips met in an explosion of joy that drove everything else out of her mind. She clung to him, feeling as if she'd finally come home, finally found what she'd been looking for all her life.

A loud tsking sound eventually penetrated the haze of passion engulfing them and they reluctantly moved apart. From the doorway, the little photographer managed to beam at them and look disapproving at the same time. Amanda's smile was radiant.

Russ fished in his wallet for a five and handed

it to his daughter. "Go buy yourself some lunch. We'll meet you in the food court in a few minutes."

Giggling, Amanda complied with his wishes. Alexa likewise made herself scarce.

"Before you can ask," Tory said the moment they were alone, "I intend to quit my job. I'll find work closer to home. I never really wanted to leave anyway."

"And Amanda? You're all right with the idea of becoming her stepmother?"

"More than all right, now that I know she can accept me." She flashed him a bright, laughing smile. "You have to adopt Dick and Pat."

"I think I can handle that."

"Anything else we need to settle, besides picking which pictures we want Alexa to print?"

A devilish light came into his eyes. "There is one thing. Has to do with a promise I made after I disappointed my family by eloping with Amanda's mother."

"A big wedding if you ever remarried?" Tory guessed. "Fine with me." A June wedding, she thought. Very traditional. At the Sinclair House.

He shook his head. "Not just a big wedding. One in which both my father and brother can . . . take part."

She had an inkling of where this was headed and groaned aloud, but her heart was too full of joy to deny Russ anything. "You want bagpipes played at our wedding, don't you?"

He nodded. "Gordon and our dad, in full regalia. And Gordon will also be my best man."

"So, that means I'll get to see you in a kilt too?" She could picture it, Russ in a kilt and a pirate shirt. She liked what she saw in her mind's eye.

"Done," he said, and held out his hand, reminding her of that first day he'd come to her door to ask for her help with Amanda.

"Done," she whispered.

She made no attempt at a businesslike shake this time. No quick clasp and release. When she touched her fingers to his, she held on, as she intended to hang on to Russ for a lifetime.

Her lips curved upward at the thought. She let everything she was, everything she felt, and all that they would become together shine through in the very special smile she bestowed on the man she loved.

THE EDITOR'S CORNER

It is with much regret and a heartfelt sadness that I offer you a glimpse of next month's LOVESWEPTs, the last treats we will be able to present to you for the holidays. The December books will be the final romances published in the LOVESWEPT line. Savor these special holiday gifts from four of your favorite authors. Like every book we've published, they are truly keepers.

In the final chapter of the Mac's Angels series, Sandra Chastain brings you what you've been waiting for. LOVESWEPT #914, **THE LAST DANCE**, is Mac's very own love story. What would it take to get Mac to leave his secret mountain compound, Shangri-la, where he runs Angels Central? A chance to meet Sterling Lindsey turns out to be too much of a temptation for him to resist. Working for Mac's friend, Sterling has had enough contact with the mysterious head of the network of angels to know there's something special about him, something that draws her to him. On the way to their meeting she finds herself in mortal danger, and her faith in Mac is put to the test. Forced into hiding, they confront emotions they'd never dared confess. In this story of risk and romance, Sandra sends a lonely hero into the greatest battle of his life: to save the woman who'd kept his hope alive. Don't miss the outcome when the man who's played angel for everyone else finds his own bit of heaven.

Mary Kay McComas knows that simple pleasures are the best life has to offer, and she reinforces that idea in **BY THE BOOK**, LOVESWEPT #915. Ellen Webster is a self-described nice person. It's when she decides she's too nice for her own good that things begin to go awry. With assistance from a little self-help book, she sets out to reach for the stars, to go for the gusto in life . . . and Jonah Blake represents gusto with a capital G. The man everyone in town has been talking about has been watching Ellen with avid interest. While Jonah is minding the town's camera store for his ailing father, he can't keep his attention away from the beautiful redhead in the bank across the street. When Ellen and Jonah finally meet, it seems as if they're playing right into destiny's hands. But Ellen begins to worry that he's falling for the wrong woman—the New Ellen. In this wonderfully touching romance, Mary Kay teaches us once again that it isn't always necessary to reach for the stars when everything you could ever want is right here on earth.

No author captures the flavor of the South better than Charlotte Hughes, and **THE LAST SOUTHERN BELLE**, LOVESWEPT #916, is quintessential Charlotte. Heroine Annie Bridges had all the advantages growing up, but her father controlled her every move. When he handpicks a husband for her, Annie decides to show her rebellious side . . . and she chooses a fine time to do it—on her wedding day! She steals her father's limo and races off in her gown, not realizing until she's fifty miles out of town that she hasn't a dime to her name. Enter the hero, Sam Ballard, an attorney/business owner who is talked into giving Annie a job as a waitress at his diner. Annie is the worst waitress he's ever employed— and the most attractive. But after working closely with her, Sam discovers she has hidden talents for accounting and sales . . . and a few of a more intimate nature. Annie can't envision life with a confirmed bachelor such as Sam, but life without him is a bleaker prospect. As they begin to fall for each other, the past catches up with Annie, and she faces the toughest choice of all. Charlotte is sure to make you laugh through your tears with this, her final LOVESWEPT.

It is fitting and appropriate that we end LOVE-SWEPT with a romance by Fayrene Preston. Fayrene was among the six authors whose books were featured in our first month of publication, way back in May 1983. She has touched the hearts and minds of so many thankful readers that there was no question who would write the very last LOVESWEPT. And what a book it is! Ending her Damaron Mark series, Fayrene treats you to **THE PRIZE**, LOVESWEPT #917. With his cousins Sin and Lion happily paired off, Nathan is the last eligible Damaron. In Paris on business, he goes for a walk and is startled beyond belief when a beautiful woman runs up to him, throws her arms around him, and says, "Would you mind kissing me as if you're madly in love with me and are never going to let me go?" Of course, he complies with her request, but when she runs off with only a thank-you, Nathan is mystified . . . and intrigued. Before he can search for her, she shows up again, this time with an apology and an explanation. When Danielle Savourat discovers the man she kissed as part of a game is a Damaron, she realizes she must clear the air. What she doesn't realize is that Nathan has no intention of letting her get away this time. Fayrene sets a steamy course for these lovers as they learn what can happen with just one kiss.

With thanks and gratitude for your loyalty to LOVESWEPT,
All best wishes,

Susann Brailey

Susann Brailey

Senior Editor